Gertie Milk
& the Keeper of Lost Things

Featuring . . .

Robot Rabbit Boy
as
Robot Rabbit Boy

SIMON VAN BOOY

RAZORBILL®

RAZORBILL®

An Imprint of Penguin Random House LLC
Penguin.com

RAZORBILL & colophon is a registered trademark
of Penguin Random House LLC

ISBN 9780448494586

Printed in the United States of America

1 3 5 7 9 10 8 6 4 2

Interior design by Eric Ford

"Welcome to your life.
There's no turning back...."

—Tears for Fears

This book is dedicated to

_____

for bringing light to dark places . . .

. . . and to my wife, Christina,
and our daughter, Madeleine.

1

Lost on Skuldark

THE GIRL LYING MOTIONLESS on the sand suddenly opened her eyes. The tide had come in and she was drowning. Waves rolled over her face then carried her up the beach, as she gasped with the shock of freezing water. When the girl was able to stand and scramble up some loose stones—away from the incoming tide—panic took over, as she realized very quickly that she did not know *where* she was or even *who* she was.

It was as though the sea had washed away everything about her life, leaving only her body—which trembled with cold, as she stood there in a wet, baggy gown with thin cloth shoes on her feet.

The girl looked frantically around and wondered if she should call out. Start screaming for help. But there was nobody. She was alone.

With the absence of sudden danger, the girl calmed a little. Her breath resumed an even pace, and her heart sank back down in her body, where she could no longer feel each thump like a stone against the wall of her chest.

She collapsed on some dry rocks and looked out to sea. The spot on the beach where she had woken up was now underwater. All around there were boulders covered with slick sea grass, like the wet fur of some once-terrible creature that had not risen for a thousand years.

Farther out, a white mist unfurled over the dark water like creeping breath.

There seemed to be no escape. The beach was enclosed by tall cliffs that erupted from the shore and stretched as high as she could see.

The girl wondered if she had banged her head, and fingered her scalp for bumps or the jagged edges of a scab. But she didn't feel like there was anything wrong with her mind. All her thoughts seemed to stick—but behind each question was a darkness from which she could pull nothing.

She looked carefully at her sopping, ragged gown for any markings or labels sewn into it. That's how she found out her name was probably Gertie Milk.

"Strange . . ." she said, rubbing the small letters sewn into the fabric, "I remember *milk* is something white you can drink, and that Gertie is a girl's name, but as to how old I am, or where I was born, or why I'm here . . . I could be anybody—or nobody."

Her missing memories might have been close, just a few thoughts away, but trying to remember felt like going around a corner that never ended.

Gertie's throat was so dry from thirst she felt the sides when she swallowed. But she somehow knew that a person can't drink seawater, because it's full of salt, and the taste of it makes you feel sick.

As the rising tide splashed over her feet, Gertie crawled backward over the stones. The entire beach would soon be deep underwater. She needed a path that would take her up the cliffs to safety.

It was painful to walk on the loose rocks, but Gertie decided she would rather have bruised feet than drown. When the rolling mist separated over the water, she stopped and stared out to sea for any sign of a ship she might have fallen from.

I know what a ship is, Gertie thought to herself, *and I have language, yet I can't remember any particular ship, or even the name of the language I'm speaking.*

What felt most strange about losing her memory was that she had no idea how she looked. She'd seen her feet and even taken a few glances at her body under the gown, but the sea was moving too quickly for any kind of reflection. It would be some time before Gertie knew the color of her eyes, the shape of her ears, the angle of her nose, or was able to stare at the curious mark that crept over one side of her face.

《 • • • 》

When the beach came to an end, Gertie clambered onto some dry boulders and looked around for a path that might take her through or over the rocks.

The fog was now creeping along the stones, as though following her, and the tide was sweeping in faster than ever. With each breaking wave, the water pulled back with such force that Gertie could see small rocks, sand, and shells getting churned into watery fists.

Then she spotted something long and white, wedged in a crack along the rock face. Gertie shuddered at what she felt sure was a human bone, maybe a leg. She closed her eyes and took several deep breaths. She could feel the pressure of tears in her throat and a pushing behind her eyes.

But then it occurred to Gertie that she might have ended up on the beach after escaping something even more horrible than bits of a skeleton . . . but what?

She quickly scanned the cliff tops for any movement— some hairy, lumbering creature, or a horde of bloodthirsty cannibals.

If it were an island of cannibals, Gertie decided she would try and convince them she was a witch with amazing, magical powers, only she had forgotten how to use them.

Then Gertie's foot knocked something. Loose stones and a dirty white skull went crashing down to the beach, rolling to rest in an upward position as though grinning at her.

The sound echoed through the cliffs, and Gertie felt dizzy, as though she might tumble down off the rocks herself.

Then something moved in the fog. The girl with no memory held her breath as her body turned rigid from fear. It was an enormous white bird with bulging yellow eyes, and it was tearing across the beach stones toward her in great, flying strides.

2

The Worst Is Yet to Come

GERTIE SCRAMBLED DOWN THE ROCKS, but there was no use running, and turning her back upon the beast felt like the worst thing to do.

The bird let out a piercing screech and snapped its cruel beak open and shut.

Gertie grabbed a handful of stones and stood her ground, shaking with fear but determined to protect herself. Everything was happening so fast that she couldn't think. If it was time to die, Gertie knew she would go down fighting.

When the animal was almost upon her, Gertie raised an arm to protect her eyes from its sharp beak. But the bird stopped suddenly just a few yards in front of her. She stared as the creature tilted its head back and forth, as though trying to make up its mind about what Gertie could be.

"Friend!" she cried, hiding the fistful of stones behind her back. "Not food! *Friend!*"

Then, as Gertie backed away slowly, one of her shoes came off. The creature looked at the shoe, then bent forward and prodded the wet cloth with its beak. Gertie continued creeping backward, still with the small, hard stones in her grasp. But then to her utter dread, she noticed, far in the distance, a dozen more birds bounding toward her. The stones would be useless against so many.

The curious animal in front of her was still playing with the shoe. Poking and prodding with its beak. Then in one motion, it hooked and flung the soggy cloth through the air so that it landed on Gertie's bare foot with a slap.

Maybe the bird was trying to help in some way, Gertie thought. Maybe it knew a way off the beach—perhaps she could even ride on its back as they floated over the waves to safety? Its yellow eyes seemed now full of curiosity and shyness.

Gertie dropped the stones and pulled her shoe on quickly. The creature watched, nodding its head. Thick white fur covered its body, and its wings were so tiny, flight seemed more like an idea than a possibility.

Gertie knew that her only hope was to make friends with it. And so, cautiously, she reached out her hand. The creature shuffled closer, and when her fingers made contact with the soft fur on its neck the animal cooed and blinked its eyes.

The other birds arrived and formed a messy line of

staring heads behind the first creature, as if awaiting their turn to be petted.

But Gertie could see the water was still rising. Time was running out. As she stroked the animal's feeble wing with both hands, she tried to think of a way to ask for help and wondered if she should just pull herself onto its back.

Then suddenly from somewhere deep in the fog came a steady rattling of beach stones and a long, low hiss. The bird jumped back in fright, its tiny wings flapping like mad. The other birds took off in all directions, squawking and screeching and beating their useless wings. Gertie turned and bolted. After a few breathless steps, she noticed the bird was following her.

"C'mon!" she cried. "We must get away."

When they finally reached the tall cliffs, the hiss and rattle of shifting stones was so close it almost paralyzed Gertie with fear. Then out of the fog it came, right behind them, an enormous head rearing up over Gertie and the white bird.

It was a head unlike any other, one without a face—just a giant, fleshy ball of holes that sucked in air and hissed it out. At first the head did not appear to be attached to anything, but then the creature turned, sucking and hissing, and Gertie saw its long, ringed body writhing on the stones.

Without wasting even a second to scream, Gertie turned and moved swiftly over the rock face. If she could just find a foothold, it might be enough to climb out of the giant worm's reach. When she turned to check on the white bird, it was gone. Then she heard that awful noise again, air whooshing from an eyeless head. She was sure it was sniffing her out—eager to suck her into its long fleshy body, before disappearing back under the sea.

"Well it's *not* going to," she said determinedly, patting desperately over the rock.

Then she noticed something—a narrow opening barely large enough for an animal to pass through but her only hope of escape. She wondered if this hole was what the white bird had been trying to help her find.

Without turning around to check for the monster, Gertie crouched and squeezed herself through the opening and into the mountain. It was just in time, too, for as she tumbled into the darkness, the giant worm head came down with an almighty *slap* against the rock. Then a furious sucking noise—the hiss of anger at letting its prey escape.

Gertie's flood of relief was mixed with concern for her new friend, the white bird. Had it gotten away? She dared not lean out and look.

A watery choir of drops echoed though the long dark tunnel. Anything could have been waiting to pounce in the silent black that was ahead. But Gertie knew she couldn't turn back and crawled forward slowly, with only her senses and the hot thumping stone in her chest she now recognized was courage.

3

Down, Down, Down . . .

Gᴇʀᴛɪᴇ ᴋɴᴇᴡ she had to keep moving, for the cave would soon flood and she'd be trapped in the rising water. Down and down she went through the tunnel. When light from the entrance had dimmed to almost nothing, Gertie stopped to rest and realized there was something in her pocket.

She plunged her hand into the wet, scratchy gown, and removed a cold, rusty key, with twirly bits in the handle. Although she could barely see it, the key felt like it belonged to a lock in an old door—perhaps in the place she had come from? Her heart fluttered with excitement. Maybe it was even the door to her home? Or was the key even hers? Had she stolen it and become a thief? Won it in an epic sword fight or ax-throwing contest? What if she was a murderer and didn't know?

In the dim light she nervously studied the key for any

red stains, and was relieved to find only a few faint letters of flowery script that read:

$$K.O.L.T.$$

Who or what was KOLT? she thought. More than likely a vital part of her getting home,

After putting the key back in her pocket (and feeling through the fabric to check it was there), Gertie continued down the tunnel until it was so dark she could not see even her own grimy, outstretched hand. It was as though her eyes were closed, and she were moving about inside her own head, searching for the lost memories of who she was, and where she had come from.

Then the path turned steep, and she began slipping forward toward what she imagined would be some horrible doom. Perhaps another worm, or the worm's mother with a feeding hole so large you could slide right in and land on her tongue and not even realize—until you were left wondering why the ground had suddenly turned into a wet cushion.

With hands reaching, Gertie ignored the pain and stiffness in her crouching body.

When the rock got slimy, she entered a large chamber where somehow there was enough light for her to see the outline of her body in the wet gown. There was also a thunderous crashing, which Gertie decided must have been an underground waterfall.

Then the tunnel narrowed again, going down into the

earth for a long time. Gertie followed it until reaching another cave where her outstretched hands brushed something soft and mushy growing out of the wall. She flung her arms up in surprise, but slapped against more of the stuff, which hung from the ceiling like a damp, rubbery rash. It was some kind of plant, which glowed when touched and gave off enough light for Gertie to see the path ahead was split two ways.

She was about to choose the right path when there was a shuddering from her pocket. The key was vibrating. She pulled it out and continued down the right path, but soon the key was shaking so hard that Gertie's teeth were rattling as she tried to hold on. She wondered if the key was trying to tell her something, and took a few steps backward. The shaking lessened to a buzz.

When she stepped toward the entrance of the other passage, the vibration was nothing more than a light tremble. Then as Gertie crossed the threshold to the left path, the key went completely still, as though satisfied she had chosen correctly. Gertie decided that it must possess some kind of magical power and was probably trying to get her home. She studied it again and ran her fingers gratefully over the four letters that said *K.O.L.T.*

Soon the path she had chosen with the aid of the key changed from a narrow passage of rock to a tunnel where soft moss grew over the floor and walls. Now, with enough light to see the outline of her whole body again, Gertie realized she must be near the top of the cliff. And after another hundred yards or so there appeared tiny openings to the sky, small explosions of white that blinded her for a few moments after looking at them.

Gertie imagined the thickness of water in the flooded tunnels behind her. The tide would be in, and the beach she had washed up on just a silent, weightless dream of fish and currents.

It was a place she would not have survived.

4

The Fear That Night Brings

WHEN THE CLIFF finally released Gertie onto a patch of cool, windswept grass, it was such a relief she did not mind shivering with cold. She gazed up into the deep blue ocean of air, gulping mouthfuls from a chill breeze. Her chattering teeth became laughter.

On one side of Gertie was the cliff edge, while on the other, a miraculous green countryside, so lush and soft and utterly delicious that Gertie remembered how thirsty she was and felt her throat and stomach tighten against the emptiness. Far, far in the distance, jagged gray mountain peaks rose up like teeth to pierce a loose blanket of cloud.

There was a path winding along the cliff edge and Gertie decided to follow it. She thought again of the giant birds. They must have made their nests higher up, where the sea could not wash them away. When she remembered their soft, furry heads and kind yellow eyes, Gertie felt something move inside her body, as though love is a string tied between the heart and memory.

After walking for what seemed like hours, the wind began gusting so forcefully that Gertie was afraid she might be blown off the cliff. She imagined tumbling to the bottom, bouncing off bits of jutting rock. From a distance, she'd be just a speck of brown moving very quickly in one direction, arms flailing. Breathless.

By late afternoon, gray-bellied clouds darkened the landscape. Then the rain began. Gertie opened her mouth to quench her thirst, but it didn't work, so she licked beads of water from blades of grass, slowly so as not to cut her tongue. Gertie knew if she didn't find shelter soon, or at least get more water, she would be in serious trouble.

The path led toward a cluster of trees. As Gertie got closer, she realized it was a forest, into which the path disappeared. With hunger pulling at her insides, and sore, wet feet, she felt like throwing herself on the ground and beating her fists against the stony earth. Night was coming. Gertie knew she would be alone in the darkness.

"Going into any forest is bad enough," she said out loud, "but to enter *now*? When there are probably crawly things and slimy creatures—worms that suffocate children with giant sucky ends then laugh about it in worm language?"

If she *had* to enter the forest, Gertie wanted to do it with the day ahead, not behind. She reached into her pocket and wrapped her fist around the curious key. The cool metal made her feel safe. After all, it had guided her to the correct path under the mountain—the one that led outside into the cool air. This told Gertie that whatever magical force controlled the key wanted her to survive.

When she arrived at the edge of the forest, roots broke up through the soil and twisted back down into the dark earth. The wind was gusting. It tore through the dense woods, whispering leaves, and groaning ancient branches.

Gertie flopped down on a mossy tree root and went over her options. She took the key from her pocket in case it had anything more to tell her.

She slipped off one of her little cloth shoes. It was worn through from walking. Gertie noticed two holes in the sole. *Sad little shoe face,* she thought. "Want to be my friend?" But the shoe just hung limply on the end of her finger.

The strong wind was freezing and stung her cheeks. Gertie sank into her gown, unable to stop shivering. She hoped desperately that at any moment, something might happen. The key vibrating again. Or the appearance of a white bird with food or even a map in its beak.

Hours passed.

The first stars came out. Cold and hard and far away. Gertie noticed them in the puddles around her. *Every night holds many small nights*, she thought, then dipped her finger and wet her cracked, salty lips with the star water.

She wondered where her real home was, and if there was food there, and a warm place to sleep, and the voices and footsteps of people who loved her.

Soon it was pitch-black. Gertie had gathered grass and dead branches around her in order to hide.

Then she tried to keep her eyes closed. But it was difficult. She worried closing them would attract the things she wished most to escape. She imagined the sound her body would make getting dragged by the leg of a giant spider.

Gertie blocked these dark thoughts by trying to picture her parents. As she didn't know what she herself looked like, this took some effort. Eventually her imagination conjured two grown-up Gertie Milks, tall and smiling—one just a bit hairier than the other.

Maybe they had taken long boat rides together, laughing as the spray soaked their clothes. Maybe her mother used to brush her hair. Gertie imagined sitting very still, as the brush pulled gently, melting knots. Her father was probably the sort of person who laughed at anything and never got angry. And what about siblings? An older sister to show her the way and whisper secrets that only sisters could share? For a brother, Gertie conjured a boy with brown hair that flopped around on his head like a slow wave. He was a serious person, but gentle, and loyal. . . .

She tried to keep her eyes closed for the count of fifty, then a hundred, then two hundred, all the while attempting to hold steady in her mind the flickering smiles and steady glances of her imagined family—hoping their vague faces would eventually change into ones she recognized.

Gertie felt sure that if she could make it over the broad back of night to morning, she would have an entire day to get through the woods. What if home lay on the other side? She would know tomorrow. Sleep was the only way to get there. Gertie shut her eyes and began to count.

Then suddenly, between forty-seven and forty-eight, a voice spoke to her in the darkness.

"I wouldn't sleep here if I were you."

Gertie jumped up in fright, not knowing which way to run.

"Unless of course," the voice went on, "you'd enjoy getting torn limb from limb by a creature so awful that it ripped apart the letters of its own name, so that no one would know it exists."

5

Moonberries & Slug Lamps

GERTIE SPUN AROUND FRANTICALLY, but could see only the faint glow of stars beyond. Then she screamed.

"For goodness' sake stop," the voice commanded. "I've got very sensitive hearing!"

"Who are you?" Gertie cried. "Don't come any nearer!"

"Don't worry, I won't! Anyway I couldn't, even if I wanted to."

Moonlight lit up the cliff and in the pale glow Gertie saw someone very small on the path before her: a tiny man no more than a few inches high. He was waving his arms around.

She crouched down. "Is that you?"

"Yes, it's me," said the man, with a hint of shame in his voice. "I'm very small, miniscule in fact, which is not the best first impression, I know..."

"I've never seen anyone so tiny," Gertie said. "Or is it that I'm really big?"

"No, *you're* normal, as far as I can tell. The truth is, when I found out there was someone on the island, I thought I should swallow some growing spice and make myself enormous in case you were some scary intruder. But I must have gone into the wrong box under the kitchen table and ended up with shrinking spice instead. Luckily, it didn't kick in until I was already out of the cottage looking for you. Otherwise it would have taken me weeks to get this far on these matchstick legs."

"But how did you know I was here? Were you expecting me?" Gertie peered closer. "Do *you* know who I am?"

"Oh dear," the little man muttered to himself, "here come the questions. It's always the same."

Gertie got down even further to look the tiny person in the eye.

"I'm sorry, it's just that I seem to have lost my memory," she explained. "Can you at least tell me *where* I am?"

"You're on the island of Skuldark."

"Can you tell me how to get home?"

"How should I know?" the man shrugged. "You don't even know where you're from."

Gertie stared at the small figure, trying to make sense of what was happening.

"Why are you looking at me like that?" he said. "You're not going to step on me, are you? I'm getting a very negative vibe...."

"I'm not going to step on you," Gertie said crossly. "I'm not that kind of person! Or at least, I don't think I am."

"Good," said the man, "because if you squished me, you'd have to spend the night out here instead of coming back to my cottage for tea and peach cake."

"Back to your cottage? I don't know who you are," Gertie said. "You might be a cannibal."

"I'm vegetarian! And you don't even know who *you* are—what if you're the cannibal!"

"Well…" Gertie thought out loud. "Will we have to cross the forest to get to your cottage? I was almost eaten by a worm monster on the beach. I'm worried there are more in the woods."

"A worm monster?"

"Yes, a giant worm with a head of scary holes."

"A head of scary holes? Oh! You mean Johnny…"

"Johnny? He nearly ate me!"

"Don't be silly, he won't hurt you, he's vegetarian too. Did you pet him?"

"Er, no, I was too busy running for my life."

"He also likes to be tickled … if you've got a feather big enough, that is. Loves a good tickle does Johnny the Guard Worm. You met the dodos I assume? White birds? They're curious things with yellow kitten eyes and tufts of hair on their heads like funny little hats."

"Yes!" Gertie said. "One of them helped me get away from the killer worm."

"You mean Johnny," the man gently corrected her. "Well,

that's nice, I'm glad you met the gang. What a shame such interesting creatures don't exist on earth anymore. Lucky I swiped a few before they became extinct."

Gertie's mouth fell open. "We're not on Earth?"

"Not exactly, but did you know, I was making a batch of moonberry juice and I found Johnny crawling around inside a moonberry? Yes, that's right, at a time when I was very worried about people, *the wrong sort*, getting onto the island. So I began to feed him regularly with that growing spice I was telling you about, and it stuck! He's lived on the beach as a Guard Worm ever since, eating all the seaweed and kelp pods that wash in. He's in his element down there."

"What sort of place is this where you can make worms grow—"

"And shrink!" said the little man. "I've got herbs and spices for almost anything you can dream up, from pretty much everywhere on Earth you can imagine."

"So we *are* on Earth!"

"Not quite! But it's good you remember there's a watery little rock floating in space that we live on. You're farther along than most. Now, do you remember what a house is?"

Gertie nodded as an image of a cozy home popped into her head. It was small but nice, with a thread of smoke over the chimney.

"Now imagine," said the man, "that in the house there are places you can go, such as the sitting room, the kitchen, toilets, up the stairs to the bedrooms, and the attic, et cetera."

"Right," Gertie said. "Got it."

"Excellent, now *that* is Earth, the places we know about and can go easily. But where *we* are is one of the spaces in the house that no one ever thinks about—such as the gap between the walls, or under the floorboards, or under the stairs . . . are you imagining it?"

"So we're trapped in a dark cupboard in an empty house with a giant worm and birds?"

"No, no, no!" said the little man indignantly. "There is no house, it's just a metaphor. You're on the earth, but, just like in the house, there are places no one ever thinks about or goes. The island of Skuldark is one of those places."

"But how did I get here?"

Before he could answer, the little man's body started to make a fizzing sound.

"Here we go!" he cried excitedly. "HERE WE GO!" Gertie watched as he got bigger and bigger until he was normal size again.

"Excellent" he said, now towering over Gertie by at least a foot and a half. "And just in time, as the nocturnal population of Skuldark is waking up for its nightly *roam*."

He pointed toward the wild wood. Gertie turned and saw dozens of glowing lights in the trees and bushes that hadn't been there before. Some were red, some were yellow, some were very dark green.

"It would be quite a beautiful display," the man said. "If each light wasn't the beady eye of a Fern Valley millipede."

"Are they friendly, like Johnny?" asked Gertie hopefully.

"Oh no, no, no, *not* at all! The millipedes are actually very dangerous. They live in deep holes, but come out in the dark to hunt."

"Hunt what? Kelp pods?"

"I'm afraid they're a bit more ambitious than that."

"Have they been watching us this whole time?" Gertie said, edging away from the woods.

"Probably listening too, the little sneaks. Which means we have no time to waste," the man said, digging in his pocket. "Here, have a Slug Lamp."

Gertie reached out her hand for the strange, soft creature, which began to glow at her touch.

"He likes you! But you're holding him by the wrong end. That's his bottom."

Gertie flipped the slug creature over and looked into his face. "Sorry . . ." She whispered. The creature blinked a few times, and then a beam of light shot out of its rear end.

"Now follow me," the man said. "And it's best if we don't talk. We wouldn't want to draw attention to ourselves, not with millipedes stomping about."

"But," Gertie whispered, "what about the Slug Lamps? Aren't they noticeable?"

"Well, it can't be avoided!" the man huffed. "Unless you have night vision. Electricity goes a bit screwy on Skuldark when the moon is full. And we haven't had any lightning for a while to fill the energy tanks."

"Where are we going again?"

"The Keeper's Cottage. Now let's get moving, there really is no more time for questions. The darker it gets on Skuldark, the more things start to wake up."

6

The Cottage of Lost Things

IN HIS NORMAL FORM, the man was rather tall, and Gertie had to walk swiftly to keep up as he strode through the darkness, his Slug Lamp held aloft.

There seemed no end to the walking, and soon Gertie's feet were dragging. But she kept the light from her Slug Lamp on the man's shiny black shoes, and when the moon came out, the trees and bushes cast beautiful faint shadows.

Finally, they arrived at a wooden gate. The man held it open for Gertie, then led her through what appeared to be a garden piled high with various things. It was very dark. Some of the stacks were taller than the cottage. Some were in the shape of people and large animals.

When they came to a door, the man removed an old key and rattled it into a lock.

"Leave your Slug Lamp out here," he said. "Next to that moonberry bush. The slugs can't get enough moonberries—that's the secret to their luminosity."

Gertie set the creature down and watched it inch excitedly toward a low-hanging moonberry leaf.

Inside the cottage, it was warm and bright, with walls and walls of books. There was a long wooden table with old bottles, quills, animal skulls, maps, a basket of wooden balls, and (Gertie noted with a shudder) an enormous dead spider under a glass dome. Inside a wooden briefcase hundreds of different colored beetles were pinned in size order.

"Those insects belong to Charles Darwin," the man said. "He had the case designed especially. Beetle-mad he was!"

At the far end of the room was a blazing fire, with two old but comfortable chairs, and a small table in between with a teapot and an uncut loaf of peach cake.

"I was just about to have tea, when the B.D.B.U. announced your arrival and sent me out looking."

Gertie stood between a shelf of leather-bound books and the briefcase of beetles, which sat open on the long table. She was starving hungry but felt too shy to say anything—even to ask if she might sit down.

"You can look at those things later," the man told her, "Come sit in one of these comfortable chairs by the fire and have the first slice of cake. I'll heat up some milk with honey too."

As Gertie ate and drank the sweet warm milk, the man dozed off with his hands stuffed into his waistcoat pockets.

Gertie thought he had a kind face, but there was sadness in the shape of his mouth. Lines on his forehead made him look worried—even while sleeping. She wondered who he was, and where he had come from.

When Gertie was almost finished eating, the man woke up.

"I can't believe it," he said, rubbing his eyes. "Did I fall asleep?"

Gertie nodded. "I was waiting for you to wake up so I could tell you how much I like peaches. That's a clue, isn't it? To who I am?"

"It *is* a clue," the man said. "You know, I don't think I've even introduced myself, my name is Kolt—"

"Like it says on my key!" Gertie mumbled with a mouthful of cake.

"Your what?"

Just in time she realized that her key probably belonged to this man. It had his name on it, after all. What if she had stolen it from him? Or worse, what if he wanted it back? She felt the key was hers now. It had guided her, it *knew* her, she was sure of it.

"Er, oh, my *knee*," she said, thinking quickly. "I banged my knee coming into the garden."

The man gave her a long, hard stare. "What did you say your name was?"

"Gertie Milk. I think."

"You *think*? So you really don't know?"

"All I know . . ." Gertie went on slowly, "is what it says

here." She pointed to the name stitched on the outside of her gown.

"I shouldn't worry," Kolt said. "As at any moment you will most likely be catapulted back to Earth, and that will be that. It's what always happens. No one will believe it when you try to tell them where you were. You'll come to think of our time together as a vivid dream that taught you not to get on the wrong side of worms—unless they're slugs with bottoms that light up."

"I'm going home?" Gertie said, sitting up. "When?"

Kolt scratched his head. "Well, that's the thing. You should be gone by now. I don't know why it hasn't happened. Most of my other visitors disappear within moments of meeting me."

Kolt examined the name sewn into Gertie's gown.

"How clever," he said suspiciously. "Who would have thought to do such a brilliant thing. It's as though you knew you were coming and wanted to hold on to something from your other life...."

"But I'm not sure it's *my* gown," Gertie admitted, lifting her arms. The fabric was now completely dry. "Seems too big."

"That's true," Kolt said. "Or you might have shrunk a little on your journey to Skuldark—or you might be someone who just happens to be wearing Gertie Milk's clothes."

While it was true, Kolt explained, that Skuldark was not on any maps, occasionally people would accidentally stumble upon it, especially sailors who fell asleep at the helm and dreamed their way here. Usually, Kolt explained, the island had a way of flinging people back to where they had come from.

But sometimes it took a bit longer, and night would come. Those who had not been returned to the world by then would usually meet grisly ends.

Gertie felt chills as she remembered the skull and the bone wedged into the cliff.

"That's why whenever the B.D.B.U. notifies me of visitors, I always go out searching," Kolt said, slicing more peach cake, and stuffing it into his mouth. "Ifeelit'smyduty tolookafterpeopleplonkedontotheisland—" he said before swallowing with a gulp. "Plus, I enjoy having guests for the short time they're here." He put some more cake in his mouth, "Theycomefromallwalksoflife," he said, swallowing, "and history—which explains why some visitors are fascinated by the chemical composition of moonberries, while others are more interested in trying to burn down the cottage and drink my blood—but then the next minute they're gone forever, back to their lives somewhere in history, leaving half-finished sentences, a few crumbs, and in the case of a sixth-century Goth barbarian—a pungent aroma."

"So . . . what time is it here then?"

Kolt thought deeply for a moment. Then a tall grandfather clock near the bookshelves struck once.

"Ah!" Kolt said. "It's ten-thirty."

"No," Gertie said, "In time . . . what year is it here?"

"We don't have years here, Gertie. Just endless cycles of nature."

"I don't understand."

"Well, on Skuldark you can never be late . . . or too early either. Everything happens when it's supposed to. Do you understand now?"

Gertie was still perplexed, but didn't want to appear rude.

"Don't worry, you'll soon be flung back to where you came from, and that will be that."

Hearing this and having decided Kolt was kind and trustworthy, Gertie decided it was time to be honest, and reached into the pocket of her gown.

"If I'm about to disappear any second, I should probably return this. I don't know why I have it, but your name is written on the side. I promise I didn't steal it."

Kolt's eyes opened very wide, and he stood up and backed away from his chair.

"It can't be! No!" he cried. "I don't believe it!"

"I'm sorry for anything I've done," Gertie stammered. "I promise I didn't take it from you, or I don't think I did."

Kolt's shock quickly turned to exhilaration.

"Of course you didn't steal it!" he said. "It was given to you, it's *your* key. My goodness! You're here! Yippee! I can't believe you made it!" Then he grabbed a magnifying glass off the table.

"My goodness!" he chuckled, staring into Gertie's

enlarged ear. "You might be the last one, but the important thing is you made it here in one piece! Welcome, dear, dear friend, welcome to Skuldark!"

"I might be the last of what?" Gertie said. "Who am I? Please tell me before I disappear!"

"You're not going to disappear." Kolt smiled. "Definitely not. You have a Keepers' key! This is a very special day!"

He strode quickly to the wall of books on the other side of the room and began pulling volumes off the shelves. "It's just so completely unexpected!" he cried. "I mean, I knew you were supposed to come, that one day you might arrive . . . but now that you're here, I can hardly believe it!"

"So I'm not going to disappear and go home?" Gertie said with disappointment. "Like the other visitors?"

"No, you're not! Because you're not like the others—you have a key."

"But it's your key," Gertie insisted. "It has your name on it. *K-o-l-t*!"

Kolt set down a giant book and turned to Gertie. "That's not my name! It's just what I call myself. K.O.L.T. stands for Keeper of Lost Things."

"Keeper of what?"

"Lost things, Gertie. You're the newest member of the ancient order of Keepers in a hundred years—Earth years that is."

"I *am*?"

"Isn't it marvelous!"

Gertie looked at the letters engraved on the key again.

She had so many questions buzzing around her head, it was hard to know which one to ask.

"So what are Keepers?"

"Keepers are very special people. I'm one!"

"But you said your name was Kolt. . . . What's your real name?"

"I really don't know. I wasn't lucky enough to be wearing a gown with a name stitched into the fabric when I arrived on Skuldark."

"You're not from here?"

"I woke up one morning on the north side of the island at the base of Ravens' Peak, with hundreds of black birds circling over me. I was terrified."

"You said I'm the newest Keeper in a hundred years, so how long have you been here?"

"Many cycles, Gertie, but we can talk about all this once you've rested. I promise to answer any and all of your questions in the morning."

He returned from the bookshelf and flopped down beside Gertie in the other chair. The flames crackled and made their faces glow.

"I always knew another Keeper would arrive someday," Kolt said quietly. "I just never imagined it would be a little girl."

Gertie sat up straight and raised her arms. "I'm not *that* little," she said, "I just look little because this gown is so enormous!"

7

A Face in the Mirror

HER ENTIRE BODY HURT and sleep pulled on her eyes. After taking
her cloth shoes from a hook beside the fire, Gertie followed
Kolt down a narrow corridor hung with gold-framed paint-
ings, portraits, and other strange things, including a glass
case displaying a doll made out of human hair. Wooden
floorboards creaked with each step, and nautical deck lan-
terns (which Kolt said often washed up on Skuldark from
sunken ships) cast a warm glow—illuminating their way
through the mysterious cottage.

"My chambers are here on the left side of the hall," Kolt
said, pointing to a wooden door with a brass hand knocker.
"But usually I doze in one of those big armchairs by the fire."

At the end of the corridor was another door with a brass
unicorn-head knocker. On the wall next to the door was an
empty glass case with a silver plaque that read:

On the Ninth of October, 1756, the Pistol in This Case Was Stolen by Mr. Allen Hunt for the Purpose of Murder

"This will be your room."

"Thanks but I don't want a room. I want to disappear like all the others, but if that's not going to happen, then can you help me find my way home?"

Kolt smiled awkwardly. "Yes, of course, but for tonight—or until we get you home—you can stay here."

But Gertie wouldn't move. For the first time since waking up on the beach, she had no idea what to do. A solitary tear rolled down her cheek.

"Please tell me I'm going to wake up and find out all this was a horrible nightmare?"

"I *want* to say yes, Gertie...."

Her cheeks were wet with tears.

Kolt placed both hands on her shoulders, and turned her toward the door.

"Go to sleep now, and in the morning we'll make a list of all the things you remember the names for, the first step to finding out where you're from."

Still sobbing, Gertie nodded.

"Use your key to enter," Kolt told her. "And always keep your door locked. It's your private place. If I ever want you I'll use the unicorn door knocker."

The bedroom was a cheerful yellow, with creamy

white wood panels that went from the floor halfway up the wall.

"I've always liked this room," Kolt said, "the yellow and white make me think of pineapple chunks and ice cream."

"I know pineapple!" Gertie said, recalling its tart sweetness, "and I know peaches . . . but I don't know what ice cream is. That's another clue isn't it?"

"You've never heard of ice cream! Where on earth can you be from where there's no ice cream? Which reminds me, feel free to bring food in here in case you get hungry at night and don't feel like going all the way to the kitchen—where I'm sure some silly thing left on the main table such as Cleopatra's dried scorpion brooch or Captain Cook's bowl of shrunken heads would almost certainly dampen your appetite."

A bed had been fashioned in an alcove beneath some windows and looked comfortable with white sheets and a quilt. There were gray drawers built into a wall, a wardrobe that could be locked, and a room off to the side with a sink, toilet, and claw-foot bathtub. The floorboards were very wide, and a much lighter color wood than the ones in the corridor. Kolt said they had been cut from enchanted hemlock trees of Fern Valley.

"The good thing about this room, Gertie, is that with Skuldarkian hemlock, you'll be quite safe."

"You mean from beasts outside? From the worms and millipedes?"

"No, from splinters, though that reminds me . . . do make

sure the windows are closed by dusk, as many creatures are attracted to light. They think it's the moon for some reason, though what the little fools would do if they actually got to the moon, I don't know!"

At the end of the bedroom was a varnished spiral staircase that led up to the second floor of Gertie's quarters, where, Kolt said, she'd find "a desk, free-standing easel, writing and drawing implements, computer-typewriter, photocopier, fax machine—though it's just for show and not connected to anything—an entire wall of books, fiction and reference, a back wall of windows looking out over the sea, a free-standing Italian telescope from the sixteenth century, an exercise bike, a rowing machine, free weights, and a long velvet couch for daydreaming. There's no microscope, Gertie, because I had to give it back, but if you look through the telescope the wrong way, you'll be amazed."

Gertie stared around the bedroom Kolt said was now hers, and felt like an imposter—as though she was taking over somebody else's life, while hers was left hanging somewhere, vital and unfinished.

After her host had gone and Gertie was alone, she sat very still on her new bed. It was a nice room, warm and private—though the wardrobe looked creepy, and every corner of the ceiling had been webbed smooth by a different spider. She still had so many questions but knew for now she must sleep.

Before closing her eyes, Gertie forced herself to get up and use the bathroom. When she turned the dial that operated the wall lamps, she found a stranger staring back in the bathroom mirror. It was a feeling most people will never have—to see their own face and not recognize it.

But what shocked Gertie the most was not the intense gaze, or fizz of her hair—but the crimson birthmark that completely covered one side of her face.

She caressed it, wondering how she had felt about it before losing her memory. Was it something she had tried to cover with her hair? A shameful mark that had kept her inside, away from glances that drained her confidence?

Gertie wondered if this birthmark was the reason she had been chosen as a Keeper ... whatever a Keeper was. She thought that discovering such a vivid detail should have brought her closer to her real life, helped her recall something, anything, like a drop of color into something clear— but those memories seemed lost forever. The more she lived now, the stronger this new girl became, this Keeper person who fought giant worms and tunneled through mountains but was too shy to ask if she could sit down.

How long . . . Gertie thought, before this new sense of self became stronger than the one she had lost? Would it be weeks or days before it covered over what remained of her real personality, drowning out the voices of those who had loved her?

In the middle of the night, Gertie shot up in bed, damp with sweat. For a split second she wondered where she was. Then her recent memories washed over her. The falling skull and white birds galloping through the fog. The journey under the mountain. Then Kolt and the Slug Lamps. Being told she was a Keeper and that she would not be going home.

But a Keeper of what? Growing and shrinking spices? Books? Beetles? Guard Worms? Moonberries?

She got up and padded barefoot to her bathroom, locating the toilet without turning on the light.

Then just as she was about to return to bed, she heard a faint *tap, tap, tap.*

It was coming from under the tile floor. She kneeled in the darkness and laid her ear upon the cool ceramic. There it was again. A tapping deep underground. For a split second she imagined the earth churning with insects, like the millipedes at the edge of Fern Valley. Perhaps one had gotten under the house, and was wrapping itself around the pipes, gnawing at them with its teeth?

But then she heard it again, and Gertie felt certain it wasn't some insect, as there was a pattern to it, a sort of rhythm to the tapping—an intelligence even.

She looked for the biggest pipe in the bathroom, then rapped on it with her hand. But her fingers were too soft, so she got her key from the bedside table and struck the pipe loudly five times. *Tap, tap, tap, tap, TAP!*

Nothing happened, then moments later she heard *tap, tap, tap, tap, TAP!* in the same pattern. Gertie tapped seven times, and then, after a moment, seven taps echoed back from somewhere deep under the floorboards.

Suddenly there was a violent knocking on her door

"GERTIE! GERTIE! It's me, Kolt! Are you there?"

She rushed out of the bathroom and opened the door to find Kolt standing before her in a panic.

"Phew!" he exclaimed, wiping his forehead. "I thought you'd been kidnapped by the thing under the cottage!"

"What thing?"

"That thing making all that noise under the floor! I'm not sure exactly what it is yet. I'll have to investigate. But I warn you, it may not be human."

"But it can count," Gertie said, holding up her key. "I've been testing it."

Kolt nodded, "If you say so. I just hope we're not dealing with Losers."

"But if someone's trapped under the house it's not their fault."

"Not losers, Gertie, *Losers* with a capital *L*," Kolt said. "And they don't deserve anything but scorn. They're a group of very, very nasty people. Their mission is to create as much loss in the world as possible. It's one of the reasons I got Johnny, the Guard Worm, in case any Losers found their way to Skuldark."

"But what if I'm a Loser?" Gertie asked.

"Well, you have a key, which makes you a Keeper. Losers can't be Keepers. In fact, they're the exact opposite. Now, go back to bed while I get to the bottom of this tapping."

Gertie folded her arms. "I want to come with you."

"I'll give you the basement tour tomorrow, Gertie, as it's, well . . . rather a lot to take in."

"Maybe I can help?" she said, secretly wondering if the

person (or thing) tapping was trying to signal her, as though it knew who she was, and where she was from.

"Help?" Kolt said, thinking for a moment. "The real question is, how brave are you feeling?"

"I'd rather be with you than left alone up here."

"I suppose if you're to be the next Keeper, there's no point putting it off."

Kolt disappeared for a few moments, then reappeared with a pile of clothes.

"I picked these out from the Sock Drawer."

"What's that?"

"I'll show you later. Get dressed and I'll meet you in the kitchen."

Gertie could hear him racing around the cottage as she changed into a pair of black denim overalls and gold high-top sneakers with a sole that lit up neon green whenever she took a step. The tapping sound under the cottage was now a frantic banging that echoed through the pipes—as though whatever was going on had gotten much, much worse.

When Gertie got to the kitchen, Kolt was wearing a black bowler hat and gulping tea.

"There you are, Gertie," he said, setting down his mug and sweeping a floor rug to the side with his shoe. Underneath was a heavy trapdoor Kolt lifted open to reveal a steep stone staircase.

"Down here, quick! Follow me!"

8

What Lives Beneath

KOLT WAS MOVING SO QUICKLY that Gertie stumbled and almost fell down the stairs. The passageway must have been carved directly into the cliff, because the walls were made of rock, and the staircase was very narrow.

"How deep does this basement go?" she asked, afraid that Kolt was taking her into the mountain again.

"Well, it's a bit more than a basement, Gertie, you'll see...."

Stone hands along the rock wall gripped flickering torches. And with each step, Gertie's sneakers turned everything neon green.

"What a bright *sole* you have!" Kolt chuckled. "Those shoes will come in handy if you run into New England witch hunters or the Goliath frogs of Cameroon during mating season."

Gertie touched one of the stone hands to make sure it was not real.

Down and down they went until reaching an enormous cavern, lit by orange cubes attached to the wall.

"Nice to see the power is back on; otherwise we might have had to run back upstairs for Slug Lamps."

The cavern was circular, and at least twice the size of the cottage. On all sides were narrow corridors, and down each one, rows and rows of doors as far as Gertie could see.

"What's behind all those doors?" Gertie asked, hoping Kolt was not going to describe something with more than two eyes, or sharp teeth.

"You'll find out soon."

In the middle of the cavern, neatly arranged in stands, Gertie saw bicycles, ice skates, skateboards, a black motorcycle with a yellow headlamp, wooden skis, a golden jacket with wings, spiked shoes attached to rope, and a giant bubble in a sort of orange rubber claw that Kolt said was a personal submarine.

"All lost objects that may have to be returned someday," Kolt said, "but until then, they help get me around down here—especially when I'm in a hurry."

"Even those?" Gertie said, pointing to the wooden skis.

"Oh, those marvelous things were made in Norway from hickory trees for an expedition to the North Pole. Luckily for the explorers, there were nineteen other pairs that didn't go missing. I need them down here for when the *ice* comes."

"Ice?"

"Yes, when the sea freezes and it snows inside the cliff."

Gertie tried to imagine the cave under a blanket of white powder.

Just then a small yellow light appeared far away in the darkness and came toward them quickly.

"Finally!" Kolt said with relief. "Ever seen a cave sprite, Gertie?"

"What's that?"

"They live down here in a hive and help me find my way about."

When the cave sprite got close, Gertie could see it was a ball of light about the size of an apple. It hovered there, as if waiting for instructions.

"Can they speak?"

"No, but they understand perfectly well, and communicate directly with the B.D.B.U."

"What's that? You mentioned it before?"

Kolt ignored Gertie's question and cleared his throat to address the cave sprite. "There seems to be something down here that's making tapping noises!"

The glowing ball didn't move. Kolt winked at Gertie, "There are seven cave sprites in total, Gertie, the souls of great warriors I believe, from a Japanese samurai to the fierce queen of Ndongo. But it's difficult to know who is who, so I named them after the days of the week. This one's a bit deaf, so I'm guessing it's Sunday, the eldest."

"SOMETHING IS LOOSE, SUNDAY!" Kolt bellowed. "CAN YOU FIND IT FOR US?"

The little ball of light shivered, then zipped off.

"Stay close!" Kolt said as they hurried after it.

After racing down several corridors with numbered doors on either side, they came to a rope bridge.

Kolt warned Gertie to cross very slowly and not look down.

"Why is there a rope bridge down here?"

"The floor collapsed in this part of the cliff about two hundred years ago, according to the records—must have been an ancient air pocket. It happens from time to time."

They were halfway across when Gertie's legs started trembling uncontrollably. "Er, how far is it to the bottom?"

"About a day," Kolt said. "Two at most."

Her palms went sticky on the rope. "Just . . . put . . . one . . . foot . . . in . . . front . . . of . . . the . . . other," she reassured herself.

But then the bridge began to swing, and panic flapped its wings inside her.

"What's that? The bridge! We're going to fall!"

"Just a slight breeze!" Kolt said. "We must be approaching the midpoint."

"Just . . . one . . . foot . . ." Gertie said, trying to control her breathing and move her hands along the rope in concert with her feet.

Finally they made it across. Gertie felt like kissing the ground, but the cave sprite was doing slow circles around her head.

"I think Sunday has forgotten where we're going," Kolt

explained, "but that's old age for you." He turned to the elderly sprite. "SOMETHING IS MAKING NOISE DOWN HERE, SUNDAY, YOU WERE TAKING US TO THE PLACE!"

The glowing ball bounced energetically, and the chase resumed down another steeply descending corridor with Kolt and Gertie close behind.

"How many rooms are there down here?"

"945 bedrooms. Now keep moving."

"945? Bedrooms? What's in them all?"

"I'll explain tomorrow," Kolt said, wheezing for breath, "when we're not dealing with noisemakers."

"Does all this have something to do with that key? With being a Keeper of Lost Things?"

"Yes, of course—LOOK OUT! GERTIE, GET DOWN!"

9

The Admiral and a Jewel Thief

GERTIE DUCKED QUICKLY, as something whistled over her head and hit an old, hollow water tank with an ear-shattering clang.

Then another object hurtled through the air and knocked Kolt's bowler hat off.

"What was that? Are we under attack?"

"Tennis balls, Gertie!" Kolt cried, shielding his face.

"What?"

"Yellow balls used in a game that's popular with people on Earth who have too much leisure time. Let's try to get closer."

As they crept on all fours, keeping low to avoid the tennis balls, the clanking became louder than ever.

"What's that thing the balls are hitting?"

"It's an old water tank that fills up if the sea level rises and tries to flood any of the rooms."

Gertie suddenly glimpsed something.

"Look! Is that an arm?"

"Where?" Kolt said. Gertie pointed to where an elbow was visible in the glow from a wall lamp. "Oh yes, I see it too. Yes, it's an arm, and it appears to be holding a tennis racket."

Gertie couldn't believe there was somebody living in the cliff under Kolt's cottage. Then a gruesome thought crossed her mind. What if this was some kind of prison? A colony of bedrooms carved into a cliff under a cottage? What if Kolt were some sort of warden? Was that what it meant to be a Keeper? She shuddered thinking about what or who else might be lurking behind the hundreds of numbered doors they had already passed.

"I've got to hit the hand," Kolt said, "so that it drops the racket."

Kolt picked up a tennis ball and tossed it at the arm, missing by a few feet.

"Why not ask nicely for the person to stop hitting balls at us?"

But before Kolt could answer, the arm moved out of the shadows, and Gertie could see that it wasn't attached to a body. It was simply a human arm holding a tennis racket that ended cleanly where it *should* have been connected to something.

Gertie screamed so loudly when she saw this that the arm dropped the racket in surprise. Kolt rushed forward, scooped up the racket, and used it to smack the arm back into the room it had escaped from. Then he threw in the racket after the arm. But before he could shut the door, a human hand adorned with diamond rings came flying out, wielding some kind of metal tool like a tiny sword. Kolt yanked the tool from the bejeweled fingers, threw it to Gertie, and booted the hand back into the room. Without a moment to lose, he slammed and locked the door with a key that was identical to Gertie's.

"Brilliant, Gertie! You were marvelous—great catch. I really have to hand it to you, ha!"

It had all happened so quickly. Gertie stood there with the small metal tool in her hand, wondering what else lived behind the doors.

"That's a lock-pick," Kolt said, taking it from her and putting it under his bowler hat. "A tool of thieves, in case you were wondering."

But Gertie didn't care what it was. "Why are there body parts playing tennis under your house?"

"Oh, that's easy to explain," Kolt said as a new cave sprite appeared to guide them back. "The arm belonged to Admiral Barbarossa, and was fashioned from pure silver sometime in the sixteenth century. Quite ingenious, but as he only ever used it for sword-fighting in the desert, it's probably good it went missing."

"But the hand with the jeweled rings—was that also fake?"

"Flesh and bone as far as I can tell. It probably belonged

to a famous jewel thief who lost it in the act of picking a lock, so that the hand and metal pick ended up here on Skuldark."

"Chopped off?"

"Most likely, but thanks to you, Gertie, we now have the lock-pick, while the naughty hand and the admiral's arm are back where they belong in limb storage. The real mystery is where the sports equipment came from—I hope there's not another hole between rooms."

Guided now by Monday—a young cave sprite who Kolt said was still learning its way around, they made their way back through the passageways and across the terrifying rope bridge. Gertie kept her anxiety at bay by firing question after question at Kolt.

"Everything that's ever been lost from the world," he told her, "is here on Skuldark—the Island of Lost Things."

"And we're Keepers of Lost Things?"

"More than that, Gertie—we return them to the world. Each bedroom below the house contains a different type of lost object. Bedroom 254 just happens to be full of lost limbs," Kolt said. "It's been filling steadily as people lose their bits in wars, accidents, and general grossness."

"But shouldn't you try to return Admiral Barbarossa's arm? Doesn't he need it?"

"Not until the B.D.B.U. orders its return. Keepers can't just return lost objects whenever they feel like it," Kolt said.

"So the hands and arms just stay locked in the room?"

"That's right. And although I am utterly repulsed by the idea of legs hopping around in the darkness, and hands continually clapping for no reason, if the B.D.B.U. orders their return, then return them we must."

"What's the B.D.B.U.? Gertie asked. "You keep saying it, but I have no idea what it is."

"It's basically a giant book," Kolt said, then quickly changed the subject. "The last time I went down to bedroom 254, just out of morbid curiosity, I opened the door just a crack to peek inside, and was immediately slapped in the face by a pair of hands, and then kicked in the stomach by a large slippered foot before I could get the door closed again."

But Gertie felt she had to know more. "The B.D.B.U. is a book? You said last night that it *told* you I was on the island?"

"The B.D.B.U., my dear, is the brain of this Keeper operation. Think of it as a book containing not just knowledge of the world, but an experience of it—how life *feels*. The B.D.B.U. decides which lost items are important enough to return to help humans."

"Help them how? Become more powerful?"

"Less afraid, Gertie. Which makes them kinder, and as a result more advanced as a species, and more able to live in harmony with one another and with nature."

"So Keepers are trying to help people?" Gertie asked with some relief—though there was still so much she didn't understand.

"Yes! By returning objects that enable people to broaden their understanding and experience of the universe and one another." Then he leaned in and whispered. "So they might eventually discover the *grand* truth," Kolt said, straightening up and adjusting his bowler hat.

"A grand truth?"

"That death is not to be feared," he exclaimed, "but a natural—even beautiful—part of nature's cycle."

"It is?" Gertie said, remembering how she felt on the rocky beach that morning with the waves crashing in. "But I think death is the scariest thing."

Kolt stopped walking. "Being killed is scary, and not knowing where the people we love go when their bodies die is horrible, but death itself is just change. You can't see the sun at night, but you know it's not dead. It's lighting up the lives of others in another part of the same universe. When people learn to value death, they'll value life and there won't be all this squabbling for power."

"Where is the B.D.B.U.?"

"It lives in a tower on the eastern side of the cottage. I'll take you there tomorrow—but try to stay open-minded in case it's in a bad mood."

"It has moods? Can I talk to it? Is it magic?"

Kolt laughed. "'Magic' is just a word for things people don't understand, or are afraid of."

Monday the cave sprite came to a stop, and Gertie found they were back in the main part of the cavern with all the different vehicles, from wooden skis to kayaks.

"Thank you, Monday," Kolt said to the sprite. "Please let all the other sprites back at the hive know how well you guided us home from bedroom 254, and . . ." he said, looking at Gertie, "that we have a new Keeper."

Monday zoomed off excitedly.

"Is every room down here so horrible, Kolt?"

"Goodness no—though bedroom 634 is a little strange. It contains the voice boxes of all the people and animals who have suffered the misfortune of losing their voices. Thankfully, it's soundproofed with dry seaweed."

About ninety-seven bedrooms, Kolt explained, had nasty, horrible, worse-than-deadly things. Most of those rooms were reachable only by whitewater tunnels, a miniature railroad, Inuit canoe, rope swing, and—in the case of bedrooms 940 to 945, located in the lowest part of the cliff— a rickety wooden elevator to sea level, where a Victorian diving suit and helmet awaited any Keeper unlucky enough to be sent down there by the B.D.B.U.

"So how do we know when the B.D.B.U. wants something returned?" Gertie asked as they trudged up the steps to the cottage, worn out from the adventure.

"Oh, you'll find that out very soon, Gertie, and it could be anything from a supercomputer to an old hairbrush that needs to go back. But you should try to sleep now. I have a feeling we'll be called into action very soon."

10

The Garden of Lost Things

THE NEXT MORNING Gertie stared for a long time through the window beside her bed, trying to remember more than she actually could. She watched the circling birds, white specks against the hard shell of blue sky. The distant sea was calm, with low humps rolling silently toward the island where Gertie found herself trapped.

So she was a Keeper of Lost Things.

She got out of bed and stared at her old gown and cloth shoes, still on the floor where she had left them. They were both so dirty she couldn't imagine having to put them on again, but decided that she would wash and keep them in one of the drawers under her bed, as they offered the only physical clues to her previous life.

When Gertie went barefoot up the spiral staircase to the other part of her bedroom, there was a velvet sleeping couch pushed against a back wall of windows where she could peer out over the endless sea.

The silence made her feel peaceful, and she looked around at all the things, wondering if they might one day feel like hers. She also felt safe in this part of the cottage, with several doors, and even the trapdoor protecting her from the things that lived below.

But what about the millipedes, whose eyes they had seen glowing at the edge of Fern Valley? And the people Kolt had told Gertie about—the Losers? There were so many things she did not understand.

With hunger clawing at her insides, Gertie went down the spiral staircase and dressed in front of the mirror, staring at the crimson birthmark covering one side of her face.

The nautical lamps along the hallway were still glowing, and Gertie tiptoed past Kolt's door to the kitchen.

Everything was very still. Kolt's bowler hat was back on the shelf near the bookcases, and Gertie saw with relief that the trapdoor to the basement was down and the rug had been spread over it. If going down there was part of Keeper life, then she felt that being whisked off home as soon as humanly possible would be the best thing in the world.

For a second, she had the idea to go outside and throw her key off the cliff. If she lost or destroyed it, perhaps she would no longer be a Keeper and, like the other visitors, just disappear back to where she had come from? But then what would happen to the ordinary lives of humans? Would they suffer because of her? She felt pulled in opposite directions, caught between what she wanted and what she knew was the right thing to do.

Light streamed in through the window, and Gertie decided to venture outside and explore while she was alone and had some time to think.

Once in the crisp, bright sunshine, Gertie took a long, deep breath. It felt good to drink down the morning air. She looked to see if there was any sign of her Slug Lamp, but decided it was probably sleeping under the thick moonberry bush.

Purple moonflowers grew up and over the entire front of the cottage, so that from a distance you couldn't really tell it was a house at all. Kolt was right, she would never have found this place on her own, and Gertie wondered where she might be if Kolt hadn't discovered her huddled in that hollow at the edge of the woods. She felt grateful to him, but accepting this new life as a Keeper felt like she was turning her back on her old self and the people she imagined were missing her.

The shadowy stacks Gertie had passed on her way through the garden the night before had been restored by morning into real things, piled high, and spread throughout the entire garden, making it a sort of junkyard for all the lost things Kolt had told her about.

There were towers of wooden rowing boats, yellowing surfboards, pianos, a tangled knot of bicycles, circus animal cages (still with straw inside), cars, motorcycles, two-person rocket ships—and in the far distance, rusty camouflage airplanes.

It surprised Gertie that she knew so many names for things. The airplanes interested her most. She wanted to get up on the wing and climb inside to where there was a seat and controls. But it would have been impossible to find her way through the maze of narrow alleyways without accidentally nudging something so that the entire garden came crashing down like dominoes.

At the top of the cottage were two brick squares that Gertie recognized as chimneys, and at the opposite end from her bedroom, she spotted the lighthouse that Kolt had told her about. It appeared to have once been quite high, but something must have smashed the upper part, and inside the ruin left behind, green plants had grown tall and birds nested.

Gertie followed a wide path to the garden gate. It opened with a creak, and she noticed, engraved in the wood, the same letters as on her key, K.O.L.T. The path wound back around into the garden, to where enormous fishing nets hung from trees. When Gertie brushed against one, her denim overall strap stuck, so that she had to pull with all her strength to get free.

Following the main path to another part of the garden, Gertie counted fifteen carriages, the sort that long ago used to bounce along with people inside wearing the most absurd puffy lace clothing, and so many jewels that it took a team of five horses pulling like mad to go even a single inch. The fact that Gertie knew this surprised her. It was another clue, and something she should write down, along with *peaches* and *pineapple*.

Growing near the ruined lighthouse, an oak tree with bulging limbs had been hung with hundreds of scarves, which swayed in the breeze as though trying to tie themselves together.

Beneath the canopy of branches, a long table was laid out with gold knives, gold forks, spoons, bone china cups, plates, and side dishes. Gertie especially liked the plates decorated with matching unicorns, as they reminded her of the brass knocker on her bedroom door. From pooling rainwater in the soup bowls, she guessed the magnificent table had been awaiting guests a long time.

"There you are!" Kolt said, when he saw her standing over the royal banquet that (he explained later) had been missing since the year 1624. He was wearing a green velvet suit and the old, worn-out black shoes he always seemed to have on.

"You don't think I look too much like a frog in this do you?" He said. "I found it in the Sock Drawer and just love the fabric."

"It's nice," Gertie said. "If you don't mind *a lot* of green."

Kolt adjusted a sleeve. "See anything you like out here among all this stuff?"

"The airplanes." Gertie said. "The sight of them makes me feel happy for some reason."

"So you remember what airplanes are!"

Gertie nodded. "I seem to remember many names of objects, but not whether I've ever used them."

"We've all been through it," Kolt admitted. "I used to try to remember my parents' faces, but I'm afraid they're more real now in my imagination than they ever could be in the real world."

The thought of never finding out who she was made Gertie want to scream with frustration. How could he give up on his family so easily? She opened her mouth, determined to tell Kolt that unlike him, she was going to get away from Skuldark.

"But now that I've got you, maybe things won't feel so lonely from now on," he suddenly admitted.

Gertie swallowed the angry words, realizing how hard it must have been for Kolt to be alone before she arrived. Perhaps if she helped him return all these things, they could both go home?

"Were you always by yourself?" Gertie asked. "Or was someone here when you arrived? Who taught you to become a Keeper?"

"A kind, fierce woman in a large black dress named Mrs. Pumble." Kolt smiled. "She liked to wear feathers in her hair, which I must say really suited her."

"And where is Mrs. Pumble now?" Gertie asked, imagining for a terrible, quick moment that she was locked up in one of the rooms downstairs. But Kolt seemed too nice to do such a thing—unless there were Keeper rules he had to obey . . . and Mrs. Pumble had broken one of those rules. "Did she find her way home?"

"Actually, yes, Gertie, she did—but when she was much younger."

"What?!" Gertie was in shock. "So then it's possible?"

"It *is* possible, but unlikely."

"I thought you said it was impossible!"

"I probably said that," Kolt admitted. "But Mrs. Pumble found her way back and stayed for two months, then returned to Skuldark."

"Why?"

"You'll have to read the book she wrote about it, Gertie. It's lying around somewhere, *Mrs. Pumble's Journey Home.*"

"I want to read it!"

"You should, because it goes into great detail about her experience, which happened long before I appeared on the island as a shivering wreck at the base of Ravens' Peak—though it doesn't say how she found the way."

"Why did she come back here?"

"It's in the book, Gertie. She even drew pictures."

"So she found a way to leave Skuldark and go home, but then decided to come back, only to disappear years later?"

"That's right. She just vanished one day, after decades of us living together in the cottage."

"So will you disappear?" Gertie asked, suddenly afraid. There was no way she wanted to be alone on Skuldark.

Kolt fixed Gertie with a hard stare.

"I'm going to be completely honest and tell you that one day, probably many years from now, I may indeed disappear, and you'll be on your own, just like I've been—unless more Keepers arrive."

"I don't want you to die!"

Kolt laughed. "It's not like that. . . . And remember, what most humans think of as death," Kolt reminded her, "is completely wrong. The sun lights up the room for a few beautiful moments . . . then travels on."

Kolt reached over to the table and picked up a bone china teacup with a gold rim. "Remember, the human body isn't the start of life, it simply holds it for a moment, the way you can fill a cup with water from a slow, deep river. Even if you empty the cup, the river flows on, and the water becomes rain, or snow, or mist. . . ."

Gertie tried to make sense of what Kolt was saying. "So if more people understood this, there wouldn't be so many wars and battles and struggles for power?"

"You understand perfectly, my dear Gertie."

But even though she understood it, Gertie still felt dread at the thought of Kolt disappearing.

"You must miss Mrs. Pumble."

"I think of her every day. Every single day. But enough of this seriousness, Gertie. Let me show you the kites. That will cheer us up."

Streaming in the distance high above the cottage were hundreds of colorful kites, snapping in the stiff breeze, their strings all tied to the same giant stone hand of an enormous, angry-looking statue half-stuck in the ground.

"Don't worry about him!" Kolt said, poking its stone eye with his finger. "He's been here as long as I have and never so much as blinked an eyelid. I assume you missed the swords, lances, spears, and deadly blowpipes on your little garden adventure this morning? You must have missed those or you wouldn't be here talking to me, ha ha!"

"I don't remember seeing any weapons. . . ." Gertie said.

"The Russian rocket ships? Umbrellas? Shrunken heads? Telephone booths?"

"Well, I might have seen a . . ."

"Shrunken head?" Kolt interrupted. "Dear child, please tell me you didn't bring it with you."

"No, but I think I saw a rocket, if that's what the tall metal things are with round windows, and I saw the giant fishing nets that are strung up everywhere."

"*Those aren't fishing nets!*" Kolt cried. "They're giant killer spider webs from the Amazon!"

"Oh," Gertie said, pulling a thread of killer spider web from her pant leg. "That must be why my overalls kept sticking to them."

"Yes, they really are awful things. I'm glad the B.D.B.U. hasn't asked me to return any of them. How they came to be lost I can't even imagine.

"To be honest," Kolt said, "it's been something of a disaster since the Age of Disappearance began, about the time I appeared on Skuldark. There used to be far more of us, a dozen or so Keepers in the old days—not only living here in the cottage, but across Fern Valley where the ruins are. You're the first Keeper to appear on the island in over a hundred years. Apart from me of course."

"But why?"

"I don't know. They just stopped coming, hence the Age of Disappearance."

"Or they didn't want to come." Gertie said, wishing she had been given the choice.

"I don't know why, but with so few Keepers left to return things, the B.D.B.U. has gone bonkers by collecting more objects than I could ever hope to return by myself, filling the rooms below—and now the garden. I don't think it knows what it's doing anymore. Not long before you arrived, a collection of French war cannons appeared in my vegetable patch!"

"Cannons?" Gertie cried. "That shoot giant balls?"

"Let's write that down," Kolt said, "it's another clue. Anyway, the cannons minced the strawberries and smashed all but three of the cauliflowers to crumbly bits."

Kolt went on to describe how the cannon*balls* had appeared in the kitchen, which was most inconvenient as getting bread to the fire on the toasting fork now required stepping madly from ball to ball in a sort of wild dance, with the added danger of losing (and possibly toasting) an eye.

Fortunately, soon after, the B.D.B.U. announced that the cannons and the dimpled cannonballs were to be returned to nineteenth-century France right away so that Napoleon

Bonaparte could get on with whatever nasty business he was up to.

Kolt explained that there was no telling when the B.D.B.U. would decide an object needed to be returned—except that it was always the *right* moment to keep things moving in the best possible direction for humans. It was a Keeper's job to be dutiful, and not to try and get out of it. Particularly urgent cases required Keepers to begin the process of return immediately.

"C'mon!" Kolt said, taking off suddenly in one direction. "Let me show you the war birds you liked so much."

As Gertie caught up under the stone archway of a half-lion, half-woman statue, Kolt was still lamenting the abundance of lost things. ". . . I am *so* ashamed of how things have piled up. But it's been just me for so long now." He stopped and looked around. "What a disaster! Not to mention, Gertie, the rare perennials *I've* lost under all this stuff!"

"Maybe I could help return things until finding a way back home?"

"That's very kind, Gertie. But even with the assistance of another Keeper, there's just so much. The B.D.B.U. has me returning five or six times as many objects as when Mrs. Pumble was here—ah, but here are the war birds!"

Gertie sprang ahead with excitement, knocking on the hollow metal wing of a World War II fighter plane.

"Well, get inside if you want," Kolt told her. "Anything that's lost is ours to enjoy until it has to be returned.

"The fact is . . ." Kolt went on, clambering onto the wing

of a 1943 Spitfire while Gertie climbed into the cockpit, "even with hundreds of bedrooms that go down and down into the cliff and under the sea, our cottage is running out of space, which explains why holes are appearing between the rooms, and things like tennis rackets are getting into the wrong hands, literally!"

Kolt sat up on the wing, making the aircraft bank slightly to one side. "Don't you agree, Gertie?"

But before she could answer, his weight shifted again, and the old fighter plane banked hard. Gertie instinctively grabbed the control ring, accidentally pulling down on the pneumatic twin-gun firing button, which sent several antique bullets crackling through the sky toward the vegetable garden, where each bullet scored a direct hit with Kolt's three remaining cauliflowers.

Gertie sat there with her hands shaking.

"Well," Kolt said, climbing out of a bush and brushing leaves from his green velvet trousers, "there'll be no vegetables until next season—but at least we can say you're an excellent shot."

"You're not mad?" Gertie said, scrambling down from the cockpit.

"Mad? Not really," he admitted, pointing at his stomach. "Cauliflowers have always made me a bit gassy."

"I do want to help," Gertie said, as they strolled back to the cottage, "but I'm afraid I don't know the first thing about how to be a Keeper."

In the sky above, heavy gray clouds were moving quickly toward them from the north, with rumbling and flashes over the darkening landscape. A close crash of thunder made Gertie jump.

"Funny you should say that, Gertie."

"Why?" she asked, wondering if it had anything to do with the almighty storm that was about to break. "What's going on?"

"It's the B.D.B.U. We're being summoned for an immediate return!"

11

Gertie Meets the B.D.B.U.

ONCE SAFELY IN THE HOUSE, they hurried through the kitchen toward the fireplace. Rain was battering the windows.

"You've only just arrived! That old book can't possibly think you're ready to start returning things."

"You mean, to the world?" Gertie said. "But I can try."

"No no no! What if you get snatched? You haven't even seen the Time Cat, let alone learned how to operate it."

"Then where are you taking me?"

"To meet the B.D.B.U.!"

When they got to the fireplace, Kolt reached for a leather book on the mantelpiece titled *A History of Chickens*. He pulled it out from the shelf, and the wall beside the fireplace slid open to reveal a secret passage.

Kolt smiled, "That was my idea! To hide the entrance using a book no normal person would ever be interested in."

"But why does the secret door have to be hidden?"

"The Losers, of course! They've never managed to break into the cottage, but one can never be too safe, especially with Vispoth."

"What's that?"

"Vispoth? The Loser's totally insane supercomputer—it's the B.D.B.U.'s nemesis."

Kolt led Gertie through to a circular stone staircase that went up and up, to the very top of the tower.

"Vispoth is a funny name."

"It does sound evil, doesn't it? Like some kind of snake god."

"Is it big?"

"Vispoth is enormous—the size of a small house in fact, with buzzing and flashing lights all over it."

"Wow."

"It's the brain of the Losers—and it's capable of calculations that would take a human being thousands of years to work out with a pencil and paper."

Gertie could feel herself getting dizzy. From the outside, the ruined lighthouse rose only a little higher than the chimney. Gertie couldn't understand why there were so many steps.

"What you saw from the outside is the ruined lighthouse," Kolt explained, "which is what you're meant to see—the real tower is inside it, invisible of course." Kolt's words echoed through the stone chamber. "It goes up almost to the clouds, and is completely covered with Narcissus paint, which reflects its surroundings perfectly—making the visible suddenly invisible. Don't ask me where Mrs. Pumble got the stuff, probably the twenty-fifth century."

Gertie wondered if the B.D.B.U. could speak, and if she would be allowed to ask a question, such as where she was from, or if her real name was Gertie Milk. She also wanted to know how they were going to return things to the world. Was there a door? Or a giant hole in the ground they could toss things into?

"How did it know I was on the island yesterday?"

"It's the most concentrated source of knowledge known to mankind, which I'm sure you know includes woman-kind, animal-kind, plant-kind, bacteria-kind, subatomic-particle-kind, invisible-kind, and of course people and creatures who are not kind at all—*nasty*-kind."

"Really?"

"It knows and feels everything, Gertie, there are even pages within the pages. Don't ask me how, but over the years bits of the book have even reached Earth and are known to humans through books and stories they consider holy or religious. But these are mere fragments—splinters from the tree of ultimate knowing. The B.D.B.U. is very old now, Gertie, and wisdom in age often comes with confusion, and a little madness!"

"I think I understand," Gertie said. "And when it wants something returned, it changes the weather?"

"That's right. Sometimes I'll wake to a light snowfall, which means the task isn't urgent at all, and after a steaming bowl of hot chocolate I'll skip up the tower steps to find out the next adventure."

"But does returning things really help people?" Gertie asked. "Maybe if you hadn't returned those cannons to Napoleon, the war would have ended."

Kolt stopped to catch his breath.

"A Keeper's task is to return things that help humans grow their knowledge. You may not know this, Gertie, but for the first 180,000 years, our species of human lived short, painful lives with lots of hair and no shampoo."

"But why did they go so long without inventing anything?"

"They were too busy, I suspect, looking for food and being chased all over the place by wild beasts. But then I'm guessing humans discovered that every living thing contains the power to regrow itself."

"From seeds?"

"Exactly, and growing food instead of always looking for it gave them more time to socialize, trade with other tribes, think and invent things like writing, so that great ideas could be written down and shared, and eventually people would live in harmony with one another and nature."

"But those cannons you returned were used to blow people up, so why did they need returning?"

"The universe is not like the inside of a clock, Gertie, where we can observe and then predict what will happen based on what *has* happened. Nature is keenly sensitive— even a tiny change can have an enormous impact, which seems like chaos but is actually a brilliant, logical pattern only the B.D.B.U. can understand."

"So most of the stuff just sits here?"

"Correct."

"We only return what the B.D.B.U. commands?"

"That's right . . . because even the tiniest thing, like an ancient copper button from the Indus Valley, can have an enormous impact on the lives of humans, but as I mentioned before, not everyone believes we're doing the right thing."

"You're talking about the Losers?"

"They want to strip the world of ideas, and destroy all technology so that humans can start again—having made such a mess of things. That's why they're trying to stop us, Gertie."

At the top of the stairs was a small wooden door with palm prints embedded in the wood, along with words:

SINT SEMPER PEIORES RES IPSAE

As Kolt read the Latin inscription, the handprints glowed.

"One for you, and one for me," Kolt said. "That means the door recognizes you as a *real* Keeper, which I never doubted of course."

Gertie followed Kolt's example and placed her hand into the smaller of the glowing handprints. It was a perfect fit. Suddenly there was rumbling—but instead of the door swinging open, it rose like the portcullis of a castle to reveal another door made of steel wires.

"This is the cage," Kolt said. Then in a loud voice, *"It could always be worse!"*

"What could?"

"No, that's the password, Gertie. It's a translation of the Latin on the first door and the Keeper's code."

The metal strands of the cage separated quickly, and Kolt led Gertie into a circular room with a stone floor.

At the center of the room was an enormous rock, upon which a book the size of a bed sat open, its pages illuminated with gold and silver light.

"Behold!" Kolt announced, "the Big Dusty Book Upstairs."

12

Don't Get Snatched

"It's HUGE!" Gertie exclaimed. "How do you turn the pages?"

"You don't!" Kolt said. "But why it's being so quiet now, after all that thunder, lightning, and rain, I can't imagine. Perhaps it's pretending we're not here."

"Or just being shy?" Gertie said.

The room they were in had windows all around, but when Gertie looked out, all she could see was blue sky and a thick blanket of cloud below.

The ceiling over the enormous B.D.B.U. was not flat like most ceilings, but a rounded dome, painted very dark blue, from which thousands of tiny glowing specks, each the size of a sand grain, twinkled.

"It's a star chart," Kolt told her. "A map of distant planets and galaxies outside Earth."

"How do you get there? In one of the rockets in the garden?"

"Underground actually, through the Tunnels of Bodwin I'm afraid, which are very nasty. Now, let's say hello to the B.D.B.U."

Kolt waved Gertie up some rickety wooden steps to the rock upon which the B.D.B.U. sat open.

At first, Gertie was mesmerized by the magnificent glow. But when she looked closely, she noticed that each page not only contained words, but images too, and the pictures were moving. Bees and birds darted across the paper, landing on tall letters, and crawling into round ones. At the top of one page was a tiny frame in which it was snowing.

As Gertie's eyes soaked up the vivid colors of the living book, its pages shimmered with a deep, intense gold. The room was suddenly full of whispering voices and warm swirling air. One of the pages began to flutter, then another, and soon they were turning by themselves, quickly, but with a delicate sound. The enormous book began to rise off its stone mount.

"What's it doing?" Gertie asked. "Is it angry with me?"

"It's just showing off," Kolt sighed. "It obviously likes you, as it's never put on a show like that for me."

"What's that sweet, smoky smell?"

"It's the wood the pages were made from. Skuldark once had old-growth knowledge trees, and the B.D.B.U. was woven from the fibers of the last one, which apparently contained all the power of the others. If I remember correctly, the trees existed as one organism, with their roots linked under the soil."

"Like a family . . ."

"Exactly, connected in every way, just like humans are. Imagine one soul shared between all. As a single tree withers, another shoots up somewhere else."

The pages of the B.D.B.U. were now flipping so wildly, Gertie's hair blew back. Eventually the book slowed and then stopped at the correct pages. Beams of white light shot out, and the words seemed to lift off the page and hover in the air.

Kolt ran up the steps and looked at the bright floating words over Gertie's shoulder. But when he leaned down to read a passage obscured by the colorful illustration of a flowering tree with branches that were moving, the book let out a giant rasping noise, snapped shut, and fell back onto its stone pedestal with a thump.

"How rude!" Kolt huffed, "All the knowledge in the universe and look how it behaves!"

Gertie stroked the gnarled brown cover of the now closed B.D.B.U. "I think it's cute," she said. "Like a very, very old dog."

Kolt sighed. "Well, that's wonderful Gertie. At least you know what a dog is."

Back downstairs, the rain was a steady drumming on the windows. Kolt consulted a map with a magnifying glass, then pointed in the direction of a bookcase. "Gertie, will you please go over to that shelf? There should be some kind of tree branch."

When she got there, Gertie crouched down and saw a bundle of wood next to a small statue of a woman holding a baby.

"One of the sticks is glowing!"

"Great!" Kolt said. "Can you bring it over?"

Gertie picked it up with extreme care, then dropped it with a yelp.

"It's hot!"

"Sorry, I should have warned you! Must be an urgent case."

Gertie picked the stick up with her sleeve and carried it to the table.

"And that," Kolt said, prodding a map in his book, "Is our destination, ancient Alexandria in North Africa."

"Why is it orange?"

"Because it's the desert, Gertie. Ready for something to eat?"

"Now?"

"You're not hungry?"

"I am, but isn't the human race in danger?"

"Yes it is, Gertie—which is why we must do our very best to return everything the B.D.B.U. asks us to."

"So shouldn't we get going then?"

"We will, I just can't think on an empty stomach," Kolt said, assembling a meal of cheese and vegetables. He explained that some objects on Skuldark appeared quite

ordinary at first, while the importance of others was immediately clear. "Such as with the first microscope, Gertie,
invented around 1600 by Zacharias Janssen while he was
apparently trying to increase the power of eyeglasses for
people with very bad sight."

"That was nice of him."

"That's what I used to think until I returned the thing
and discovered he was using it to perfect an illegal coin-
making operation."

It was also convenient, Kolt pointed out, that the
stick happened to just be sitting there in a bundle on the
bookshelf.

"That buys us a little time for lunch," he said. "Most
objects have to be retrieved with the help of a cave sprite
from one of the 945 rooms beneath the cottage."

Outside, the thunder was now so loud that glasses dry-
ing by the sink began to vibrate.

"No need to panic just yet," Kolt said. "It's just the
B.D.B.U. making sure we don't forget."

"It seems angry."

"Oh it's furious!" Kolt chuckled, giving Gertie a triangle of soft cheese. "But I can tell you from experience that
traveling through time on an empty stomach is a terrible
idea."

Gertie nearly dropped the cheese. "Traveling through
time?"

"Didn't I mention that?"

"No you didn't!"

"The time machine is parked outside in the garden. You haven't seen the Time Cat yet."

"A *time machine*?" Gertie could hardly believe what she was hearing.

"Yes of course, how else did you think we got things back to the world? Through a hole in the ground?"

Then Gertie realized something. "If we have a time machine, why can't we use it to go back to our families?"

Kolt bit into a piece of green pepper. "It's more complicated than that. We can only travel to the time and place in history of the object we're returning. Plus, you don't remember when it is you're even from!"

"But after returning something, couldn't we stay awhile?" Gertie suggested. "Ask around, see if anyone has ever heard of me, or you?"

"We only get eleven hours in each place. The B.D.B.U. used to give us twelve hours but then I accidentally spilled tea on page 7,323."

"What happens after eleven hours?"

"If we haven't used the time machine to return to Skuldark within eleven hours, we get snatched by the B.D.B.U., which is best avoided as it's a slow and extremely painful way to travel. Don't ever allow yourself to get snatched, Gertie. Always, always use the time machine and your key, which operates it."

"My key operates the time machine?"

"Oh yes. Don't ever lose your key."

Just then, thunder ripped through the cottage, causing the lights to flicker.

"Yes, okay! We're leaving in a minute!" Kolt shouted through the wall toward the tower.

"Tea or moonberry juice, Gertie?"

"Er, moonberry juice, please."

Kolt took Gertie's teacup to a kitchen cupboard, where he popped the cork out of a tall bottle, and poured out bright purple liquid. "Here you are," he said, handing it to her carefully. "Just a splash until you get used to it."

Gertie took a small sip. At first, it was ice cold and didn't have any flavor. Then she felt a sort of bubbling and her whole mouth glowed with sweetness.

"Is it fizzing yet?"

"On my tongue!"

"Summer moonberries are fizziest because they grow under cloudless, glittering skies, where starlight blends with the lunar glow. By the way, did I mention magnets?"

"I don't think so."

"Well, don't go anywhere near them! Magnets are the enemy of all time travelers. For some reason, they mess everything up."

"Okay," Gertie said, "stay away from magnets."

"Yes. Very important."

"What if my key gets lost? Will I be sent back to—"

"To where you came from? No! If you lose your key along with the time machine and get snatched—you will lose the ability to travel through time, and if you're the only Keeper, that's a very big problem. *Always* remember to take the time machine and key with you at all times, and to stay away from—"

"Magnets, I'll remember," Gertie said. "I promise. I'm just happy I have a way back home."

Kolt bit into some cheese as lightning flashed at the window. "But do you know where exactly in the world you're from, Gertie? And when in time? And who your family might be? Their names for instance?"

"The Milks?" She winced, realizing he might have a point.

"I looked for my family for hundreds of years. But I don't know who it is I am looking for. I might have met them several times already and not known it."

"But they're out there somewhere. They have to be, right, Kolt? We're connected like those tree roots, remember?"

"They're out there right now, sure as you and I sit here breathing—but say we travel to Vienna in 1734 or Lagos in 1986, what if it's one thousand years too early? Or two hundred years too late? Or fifteen thousand years too early? Or ten minutes too late?"

"But if *we* are missing from the world, Kolt, shouldn't *we* be returned too? Who returns us?" Gertie said, feeling sudden anger at the unfairness of it all.

"I don't know, Gertie, but there's always a right moment for lost objects to be returned, so perhaps it just isn't our time yet. All I know is that we're bound by sacred terms to do our Keeper duty."

"Even if we didn't choose it?"

"It was chosen for us, Gertie. We didn't choose to be Keepers any more than we chose to be born."

Kolt was going for the last roasted vegetable when thunder crackled through the cottage with such force that he was thrown from his chair onto the floor. The vegetable flew off his plate toward the bookcase, landing on the statue of the woman, who now held a carrot instead of a baby.

"Come on then!" Kolt said, getting up. "Before the seas begin to boil, let's go!"

13

The Sock Drawer

THEY LEFT THE TABLE and hurried to a small, ordinary-looking door near the books.

"Welcome to the Sock Drawer," Kolt said, turning the handle to reveal a descending staircase. "Bedroom 87, home to all lost clothing."

"Is it really a drawer?" Gertie asked. "Should we go in one at a time?"

"One at a time?" Kolt laughed. "Down these stairs, you'll find a complete fashion history of the world, so that we can blend in with the locals and make our job of returning things even less dangerous."

Gertie descended the steps carefully, and soon found herself in one of the biggest and most exciting bedrooms, with racks and racks and *more racks* of clothes, shoes, and accessories from every place and time in history.

"So time travel is dangerous?" Gertie asked, noticing a tall shelf with armor and helmets.

"Not the traveling part, Gertie—oh it's bumpy on occasion, and if we take a wrong turn and end up in 2488 instead of 1488, then we just come home and wait for the B.D.B.U. to reset the time clock and try again."

"I like *that!*" Gertie said, pointing to a tall cone-style hat.

"Sorry, Gertie, that's a fifteenth-century Hungarian hennin hat, completely wrong for where we're going."

Gertie held up a dagger-staff, engraved with hieroglyphs, from a rack of swords. "Could we take this?"

"We almost never need weapons, Gertie, but it's an interesting piece."

Gertie replaced it in the rack next to a ruby-encrusted battle ax.

"The *dangerous* part," Kolt went on, "is the occasional vicious creature, or earthquake, or"—Kolt laughed—"in the case of traveling to years 4900 B.C.E., 866 C.E., and 2187 C.E.—cosmic events from meteor showers and solar bursts related to gravitational realignments—not the best time to get a flat tire. It can be especially hazardous when returning things to nether regions. To this day, I've thankfully never seen the Pits of Megatronus, the Bruggedon Tundra, the Salt River of Knapp Gorge, the Devil's Cape, the Glowing Triangle of Jig, or the famous blood tunnel of Darren Island."

In the center of the Sock Drawer was a large globe, revolving slowly.

Kolt went up to it and spoke out loud the year they intended to visit, 240 B.C.E.

The world stopped moving. Then land and water shifted into a new position and changed color.

"Clever, isn't it?" Kolt said. "Say any year, and the continents and seas shift to reveal what the Earth looked like then."

"What do the colors mean?"

"Temperature and wind!"

Then tiny numbers and letters appeared over the areas of land, each set corresponding to a particular rack of clothes.

When they arrived at rack B21, Gertie gazed over the rows of different colored fabrics. Some were woven with gold and silver, while others looked dark and foreboding.

"Nothing too royal, Gertie, as the B.D.B.U. didn't mention kings or queens on this trip. That's a good thing by the way, as most people in power are a bit batty or soon will be."

"This is nice," Gertie said, pulling a dress off the rack, "but the material is quite rough. It's like sandpaper."

"Ah! You remember what sandpaper is! Very good, that's peaches, pineapple, bicycles, chickens, the ability to operate a World War II machine gun, and now sandpaper. As for the frock, if it's what people wore in 240 B.C.E., then we have no choice. We must be fashionable—our lives depend on it."

"Does the Sock Drawer always have the right outfit, Kolt?"

"Always." Kolt smiled. "I've dressed up as a sixth-century

Australasian snake handler and a Wild West sheriff, and even an Egyptian queen. That involved the crushing of fish scales to get the makeup shimmery enough."

Gertie settled on a knee-length hooded gown in orange with black seams. She pulled it over her head and straightened the fabric. The storm outside was now like a ferocious beast with the cottage in its grasp.

Kolt knocked on her dressing room door. "Time to get some money, then it's off to ancient Alexandria to return the Persea branch!"

With rain pummeling the house like thousands of small fists, Kolt led Gertie to tiny bedroom 88 at the back of the Sock Drawer (nicknamed the Piggy Bank), which was nothing but buckets and buckets of cash in all forms from coins to banknotes to tiny star-shaped mirrors to polished stones and even vials of spices.

"You're rich!" Gertie squealed at the sight of glittering buckets of money and jewels.

"There's enough cash here to buy anything, though after centuries of shopping I've learned that the only thing worth purchasing is a fresh doughnut. I'm not joking, it really is the only thing."

Gertie watched as Kolt fished around in a bucket of gold and silver pieces for money they would need on their excursion.

Gertie pinched her nose. "Wow, this stuff really smells!"

"The secret is getting the right money for the right era, Gertie. If you don't, people get suspicious, which is extremely dangerous before 1920, when most folk weren't used to seeing strangers much. Though the era called 'prehistory' is when you really have to watch out of course, as even just showing up unannounced with fairly good teeth was a good enough reason to be burned alive or thrown into the cooking pot with a potato or two."

Gertie hoped he was joking. "Who would hurt a child?"

"The Carthaginians, for one." Kolt shrugged. "But don't worry, I'll make sure that you look the part. Now we really must hurry...."

With their pockets jangling, Gertie and Kolt rushed out into the raging storm toward the time machine.

14

The Time Cat

As Gertie stood in the pouring rain, watching Kolt fiddle with the lock of an old green car, she discovered quickly that her North African linen cloak was not waterproof.

"Blast this thing!" Kolt muttered. "Of all the times it has to jam!"

"So where's the time machine?" Gertie asked, trying not to shiver as rain lashed her bare legs. Kolt looked up from his jiggling of the door handle.

"You're looking at it," he said, extending his arms. "This is the amazing one and only Time Cat."

As if the old green automobile heard the compliment—the door suddenly swung open. Gertie and Kolt clambered inside, completely soaked.

"Despite the tricky handle," Kolt said, water dripping off

the end of his nose, "the Time Cat is quite brilliant and has only let me down 397 times."

"That seems like a lot."

Kolt chuckled. "Not for a British car, Gertie—it might even be a record."

"So now we just drive back to Earth?"

"Er, not exactly, but the fact that you know what a car and driving both are is a great clue because if you were from the 1800s, you might see this as some kind of horseless carriage, or if you'd come from the thirty-fifth century, you'd have no idea what it was—except for maybe one of those mobile, automated dental surgeries that crawl through cities searching for people with bad teeth. The fact you know this is a car tells me you're from the twentieth or twenty-first centuries, which narrows it down to about two hundred years!"

"Why do you call it the Time Cat?"

"Because it's a feline of sorts, as this particular motor vehicle is from England, where it was known as a Jaguar— which is a rather ferocious sort of cat. The *actual* time machine is nothing more than a small plain wooden box created from inside the B.D.B.U. with a space for your key. It's in the glove compartment if you want to take a look."

Gertie pushed the button, then opened the varnished wooden door. Inside she found a small wooden box, barely large enough for a keyhole.

"Take out the time machine," Kolt said. "Do you have your key?"

Gertie checked her pockets, but she had left it in her denim overalls, which were hanging up in the Sock Drawer.

"Well, never mind," Kolt said. "We'll use mine as we're in a hurry, but in the future you must never forget to bring your own key."

"I promise," Gertie said.

Kolt hesitated for a moment.

"It hurts me to say it, but a few decades ago, an inexperienced and nervous Keeper made the grave mistake of getting snatched without his key and time machine, which is why the Losers can now travel to any point in history that Vispoth decides is where they can cause most trouble."

"Vispoth is the Losers' totally insane supercomputer?"

"Well remembered, though for a long time my lost time machine and key wouldn't work for them. The B.D.B.U. must have simply shut them down—but then the Losers fed them into Vispoth and it found a way to link the multiverse compass with the graviton bridge, thus overriding the B.D.B.U. Still, the Losers can only go where Vispoth sends them."

The rain was now like a river on the windshield of the Time Cat. For a moment, Gertie thought the sea was upon them, and at any second they might be washed off the cliff. Kolt was still fiddling with the controls, pushing buttons and turning knobs.

"Is a little air conditioning too much to ask?" he shouted at the spinning dials. "Come on!"

"How are we going to drive in this weather?"

"We don't drive on Skuldark," Kolt explained. "I modified this old but rather striking *automobile* so that we could drive once we get to the other side of the graviton bridge, which connects our dimension to the dimension on Earth where the object is going."

"So will I learn how to drive the Time Cat?"

"Technically, you don't need the Time Cat, Gertie, just the time machine. Simply insert your key into the little box, put the box anywhere on your person, then within a few seconds, the B.D.B.U. sends you where you need to be.

"However . . ." Kolt went on, still pushing buttons on the dashboard of the old car. "Either accidentally or on purpose, that demented old book, every now and then, has sent me to the completely wrong place. I once showed up on the wing of a fighter jet dressed in the donkey costume of a dancing boy from the court of Queen Cassandane Shahbanu. You should have seen the pilot's face when I waved hello."

Then Kolt demonstrated how to check the Time Cat's power by tapping a round gauge with a white needle.

"Sometimes it sticks," he said. "But I've adapted the car to run on Skuldarkian seawater. If you ever forget to check the levels and run out of juice somewhere in time, grab the time machine from the glove box, insert your key into the lock, say the Keeper's motto, *It could always be worse,* and you'll be back home in no time at all. The Time Cat has a way of finding its own way home—as without the time machine, it's technically lost—though I've never worked out how it learned to park itself in the garden every time."

Just then, sparks exploded from a nest of exposed wires under the steering wheel.

"Aarggh!" Kolt shouted. "With a classic like this, Gertie, there's always something in need of fixing. Rome wasn't built in a day—though I sometimes wish it hadn't been built at all!"

As Kolt entered the time coordinates on the dashboard, orange numbers flashed on a screen in the middle of the steering wheel.

An explosion of thunder ripped the sky in two—but Gertie felt safe inside the Time Cat with the Persea branch in her cloak. There was even carpet, and a glass case on the backseat with EMERGENCY PEACH CAKE AND MOONBERRY JUICE written on the outside.

When Kolt fed his key into the tiny time machine, the Time Cat began rattling violently. "I'm rather attached to this old thing, which is against Keeper policy, but I'll explain that later."

"What's happening?" Gertie said. "Why is it shaking so much?"

"That'll be the photon relay warming up. I like to think of it more as a purring, actually...."

Then, with an intense fizzing sensation, an ear-shattering pop, more violent rattling, a scream of excitement from Gertie, and the side mirror falling off—they disappeared.

15

The Battle of Trunks and Humps

AFTER A FEW SECONDS of weightlessness, a burst of white light, the need to sneeze, and a jolt that made Gertie's head fly back, they were suddenly on the side of a mountainous sand dune.

"It worked! We're here!" Gertie cried.

Kolt opened the sunroof. "And what a lovely change in weather from all that rain."

Gertie couldn't believe the sudden heat and rolled down her window. It looked as though they had plonked down in the midst of an approaching sandstorm, as Gertie noticed an enormous rolling cloud of dust in the distance.

"What's that?"

"It looks like we're in for more bad weather, after all," Kolt said, surveying the horizon.

But as the cloud got closer and closer, Gertie realized that it wasn't a sandstorm at all but hundreds of armor-plated camels in full charge kicking up dust.

Gertie squinted and cried out. "There are people on the backs of those camels, and they're holding swords!"

"Well, technically, they're scimitars, Gertie," Kolt said, jerking the steering wheel. "See how the blades are curved? Let's head in completely the opposite direction, and maybe close your window so that we don't get sand in our eyes."

Gertie rolled up the window with the Time Cat's old leather-topped handle.

Kolt laughed. "You were right! We should have brought that dagger thing after all!"

They were soon rolling quickly over the scorching sand ahead of the furious pack, which would have been excellent, were Gertie and Kolt not *now* faced with another dust cloud—this time an impenetrable line of bronze-plated elephants, whose riders, Kolt observed, seemed about to engage with the camel army behind them in a battle of trunks and humps.

"The key is not to panic," Kolt said. "It looks as though we've accidentally landed on an ancient battlefield. I feel like some music might calm us down, don't you, Gertie?"

"Er, maybe not right now," Gertie said, as battle cries and animal noises filled the air.

"Just a little something to take our minds off it," Kolt said cheerfully.

As they neared the line of battle-hardened elephants and their crazed riders, Kolt turned a knob, and the sound of violins filled the car.

"Isn't this nice?" he said, as a barbed spear whistled toward the windshield. "I believe this piece is called 'Night Music.' It really is quite relaxing," he went on, steering sharply to the right.

But Gertie was distracted by several elephant riders who had dismounted and were running toward the Time Cat with curved swords aloft.

"Kolt, look!"

"Wow!" Kolt exclaimed, "They're not wearing any shirts? Seems like a terrible idea to go into battle topless. Maybe all that chest hair makes them feel brave."

"Shouldn't we do something?"

The riders were so close now, Gertie could see their snarling faces and crooked teeth.

Kolt couldn't believe it. "Aren't they afraid of those long beards getting caught in chariot wheels? I would be!"

"Kolt!" Gertie yelled, pinning herself back in the seat.

"There's really no cause for alarm," he reassured her, pushing firmly down on the horn with only a second to spare.

Gertie clapped her hands over her ears as an almighty roar emitted from under the hood of the Time Cat. The sound echoed through the desert. The terrified men dropped their swords and ran off screaming.

"I never get bored of that," Kolt laughed. "Every time I do it feels just like the first time."

He pressed the horn again, and several panicked elephants bucked their riders and bolted.

"I usually hate driving in crowds," Kolt said, leaning into the horn for several seconds. "But you find ways to make it fun don't you?"

"What *is* that terrible sound?" Gertie asked, keeping her ears covered.

"As I told you, bedroom 634 under the cottage is filled with voice boxes from people and animals who have lost their voices. I installed several different kinds of voice boxes under the hood of the Time Cat—this particular one is quite effective and belonged to a *Tyrannosaurus rex* with some tooth decay. But I have to admit, the wail of the Fern Valley banshee is my absolute favorite. That one scatters people like a ripped bag of marbles. Oh my goodness, it's wonderful!"

They were now dodging camels and elephants left and right.

As Kolt swerved around another pack of fighters, the sleeve of Gertie's loose gown caught on the door latch. Before she could cry out, Gertie went flying from the Time Cat onto the sand.

The softness of the desert broke her fall, but Gertie's face stung from grazing the hard grains. She jumped to her feet as the battle raged around her.

"Kolt!" she cried, dodging a spear.

"Hold on!" he shouted, trying to reverse around a camel. But then Gertie notcied a riderless elephant thundering toward her. The animal reached out its trunk and pulled Gertie onto its back. In order not to bounce off, Gertie wrapped her arms around the creature's neck as they charged to freedom.

Soon the battle was just a dust cloud on the horizon. The elephant slowed and Gertie slid down off its back.

"Thanks for rescuing me!" she said, patting the elephant's rough hide. The animal raised its trunk, then kept walking.

Gertie watched it disappear over a dune, remembering the white bird that had tried to help her on Skuldark. She wondered if she possessed some deep connection to animals. Perhaps it was another clue to who she was.

After plodding to the top of a sand dune, Gertie scanned the horizon in all directions, but there was no sign of Kolt, and she was beginning to feel dizzy from the blistering heat. She sat down, but the desert ground was scorching. It was best to stand, where she imagined the sun burning the birthmark on her face into a deeper, darker crimson.

Before long, Gertie had breathed in so much dry, desert air that it hurt even to swallow. She closed her eyes and tried to comfort herself by imagining the faces of her family. But instead she heard a voice in her head that she recognized as her own.

"Camel," it said.

Gertie listened again, trying to connect an actual memory with the sound of the word. She wondered if she was going mad from the sun. She was sure it was her own voice, but one from the past, before she was a Keeper.

Soon, she was so exhausted that her body fell to the sand. She curled into a ball and felt herself beginning to melt. In the moment before she lost consciousness, Gertie found herself wondering why the sun does not recognize human pain and is not capable of pity.

16

Incense and Elephant-Snout Fish

GERTIE WOKE TO THE FEELING of ice-cold emergency moonberry juice boxes being held against her head.

"That was a close one!" Kolt said. "I almost lost you on your first mission as a Keeper!"

"I . . . need . . . some . . ." Gertie croaked.

Kolt popped the foil opening with a straw and gave her one of the ice-cold boxes.

After several seconds of pulling up fizzy, freezing juice through the straw, Gertie felt herself flooding back.

"Are the soldiers trying to find us?" she said between sips.

"Those bare-chested maniacs are much too busy battling for their lives, or for treasure," Kolt scoffed. "Or for some queen who's convinced them that dying for her sake means some amazing reward in the afterlife—typical history really—but what an amazing spontaneous animal rescue you pulled off! That's exactly the sort of thing I want to teach Johnny the Guard Worm to do."

"Yes, but I was carried into the middle of the desert."

"Out of harm's way..."

"Except that I was almost cooked when you found me!"

"Gertie jerky!" Kolt laughed, then quickly cleared his throat. "Sorry, Gertie, it's not funny at all. There's nothing hilarious whatsoever about you turning into a snack for passing vultures."

"Something strange did happen," Gertie said, taking another drink of the ice-cold berry juice. "I heard the word 'camel' in my head, but it was a memory of *my* voice saying it in my old life."

Kolt thought for a moment. "It's another good clue, as there aren't too many places in the world where camels and humans live together."

When they were safely off the dunes and bouncing along a rough camel track, Gertie pointed out a shimmer in the distance.

"It's far," Kolt said, "but that's it . . . the ancient city of Alexandria, home to that rather unremarkable stick the B.D.B.U. seems to think is important—and the destination for your very first trip through time!"

"Apart from the one that brought me to Skuldark from my home," Gertie insisted.

"Of course," replied Kolt in a kind tone. "Apart from that one."

After a couple of hours, the desert track evened out,

and there were palm trees and low green bushes. Kolt said the temperature outside was now so high they could have cooked lunch on the roof of the car, but that it would have ruined the Time Cat's British racing green finish.

"Thank goodness for air conditioning," he said, playing with the vent. "And when we get outside, these itchy robes will keep us quite cool."

They were now rolling in and out of sandy craters, with brown stone houses and tents rising up in the distance.

"We'd better leave the Time Cat here and walk the rest, otherwise people will be clambering all over it, trying to figure out what sort of chariot it is, and then we'll be summoned to see a king or some terribly important official and, after eating a lot of tiger nut cake, be made to wash our hands, braid our hair, then wave to thousands of people in a parade."

"But where can we leave the Time Cat where it won't be seen?"

"Oh, don't worry," Kolt said, pointing to a button with a question mark printed on it. "This makes the car look invisible for as long as we want. It's not really invisible of course, just more of that Narcissus paint I told you about, the same stuff used on the tower where the B.D.B.U. lives. There are also two Narcissus bodysuits in the trunk if you ever fancy appearing invisible, excuse the oxymoron."

When they got close to the city, the road widened and became crowded with people pushing in all directions. The air was very hot and heavy with the smoke of incense.

Vendors displayed baskets of ground-up spices, shimmering rolls of fabric, and even live snakes that Kolt said people were buying to keep rats out of their grain storage. Some baskets were strapped to donkeys or camels, and some were carried on heads. Everything was dusty and almost too bright to look at.

"If we find ourselves here after dark, we'll most likely see the famous lighthouse with flames shooting out of the top! There's a library too with hundreds of thousands of handwritten books, and don't get me started on the shopping."

Gertie was more interested in the people. "What if someone speaks to us?" she asked, suddenly nervous. "I don't know Greek or Egyptian or anything!"

"Fortunately, you speak Skuldarkian beautifully," Kolt assured her. "The Skuldarkian language changes to match the place, so it's understood by everyone throughout time and allows us to understand everyone else."

"So I can speak every language?"

"With the exception of a few encrypted magical languages—Swamp Mouth for instance, the spirit-dialect of Fern Valley, and Olde Skuldarkish—absolutely any language in the world."

Suddenly a crazed mule appeared from an alley and bolted toward Gertie with a cargo of freshly ground turmeric on its back. Gertie felt someone lift her up, and the animal stampeded past with its owner in pursuit, sandals flapping.

"Another lucky escape!" Kolt said, putting her down

gently. "Turmeric stains are impossible to get out. But c'mon, it's almost noon, which is when the B.D.B.U. says this stick must be returned."

"Or what will happen?"

"I don't know exactly, actually. Things might get a bit *sticky*?"

Gertie followed Kolt past more market stalls, where there were all kinds of things to eat, from Alexandrian venus clams to dates, elephant-snout fish, pomegranates, wine-fattened snails, even vials of pink powder—medicine ground up from sea-urchin shells.

"The house is supposed to be on the other side of this market," Kolt said.

"How do you know?"

"Didn't you read the glowing words in the B.D.B.U.?"

Gertie flushed with embarrassment. "Er, I was looking at the lights," she said. "What if we can't find the owner?"

"I don't know, because I usually manage to locate the person—though not always."

Gertie wondered if she'd ever be as good a Keeper as Kolt seemed to be.

"Sometimes, I'm afraid, well, er, I've had to, well, leave an item in a mailbox, or on the person-I-couldn't-find's pillow—or in the case of a very important medieval diamond, in a sultan's satin slipper, as he was busy getting captured by an invading army."

Gertie was about to suggest that the B.D.B.U. group objects by place and time, so that multiple items could be returned on a single trip. But before she could get the words out, Kolt was pounding on a heavy door.

"We're here!" he said. "Hello? Hello? We've got your stick! Open up!"

When the door opened, a short hairy man wearing what looked to Gertie like a blue and white dress stood before them barefoot.

"No visitors! No visitors!" the man said, and began closing the door.

"But, we have—" Kolt protested.

"No visitors!"

The door slammed in their faces.

17

The Earth Is in Their Hands

"WHAT SHOULD WE DO NOW?" Gertie asked.

Kolt handed her the stick. "Time to branch out! I'll knock, and when he opens it, throw the stick in! Then we'll both run away."

"Is that what we're supposed to do?"

"The B.D.B.U. said to return the object to this location before noon on this day, but it didn't say we have to make friends with hairy people."

Kolt pounded on the door, and within a few moments they heard feet slapping a marble floor, and the door opened. The hairy man was about to shout something horrible when he noticed what Gertie was clutching.

"The stick! Master! Come quickly! The stick! The stick!"

"*The stick?*" called a voice in the distance. "The stick?"

Kolt glanced at Gertie. "Oh, I hate this sort of thing," he said. "I wonder if they're going to think we're thieves."

"What if they imprison us?" Gertie asked, trying to give the stick back to Kolt. But he stepped away.

"I don't want it!" he cried. "Children are much easier to forgive than grown-ups."

Then the owner of the stick appeared. He was middle-aged with a long dark-skinned face, graying hair, and beard. He was wearing a cloak similar to Kolt's, and sandals with straps that tied up around his ankles.

"Oh my child!" he said. "You've found it!"

"Yes, here it is!" Gertie said. "Fresh from the desert."

"*Where* in the desert?" the hairy man asked suspiciously. "I've been looking for Master Eratosthenes's stick for days."

"Eratosthenes?" Kolt muttered, nudging Gertie. "He's a famous mathematician!"

"I found it on the sand," Gertie said, folding her arms. "In the sun."

"Yes, of course you did." Eratosthenes nodded. "Now I remember! That's where I left it. But how did you know it was mine?"

"Oh," Gertie coughed, "I'm so thirsty! Got any juice?"

"Yes!" Kolt agreed, hacking away. "Me too! My throat is cracking!"

"How rude I've been," Eratosthenes cried. "Please, come in for refreshments."

"But master, it's almost noon," said the hairy man.

"Then look after our guests, while I go and get the string." At this, Eratosthenes shuffled off, waving the stick above his head.

"Is it me, or are they a bit funny?" Gertie whispered as they followed the hairy man into the luxurious Alexandrian villa.

Kolt nodded. "Very peculiar. Be on your guard."

Soon they found themselves in a marble courtyard with high stone walls that blocked out noise from the busy alleyways surrounding the grand house. Wide round pillars held up the stone block ceiling, and in the center of the courtyard was a square pool of clear water with green plants growing at the edges. The roof over the pool was open to the blue sky, and the noon sun poured in.

In one corner of the room was a golden harp on a stand, and across the courtyard, in shady areas, several peacocks dragged long shimmering trains of feathers.

Gertie and Kolt were invited to sit on comfortable beds with red cushions as the hairy man ladled fresh well water from an amphora into drinking cups. Then he brought a terra-cotta bowl of juicy grapes, a brick of hard cheese that Kolt said was made from camels' milk, and a dish with pitted olives mixed with oil, vinegar, cumin, coriander, rue, and mint.

"Eat now!" the hairy man barked. "Drink now!"

Kolt's eyes bulged at all the food. "With pleasure!"

"I thought you said to be on our guard?" Gertie reminded him, pulling some of the irresistible-looking cheese from the brick with her fingers. It had a chalky flavor with a lingering sweetness at the end.

Then Eratosthenes reappeared holding the stick and a piece of string. He rushed to the center of the house where the sun was warming the tiles around the pool of water. A peacock was fanning its feathers in the hot rays, and Eratosthenes shooed it away. Then he held his stick up, and with the other hand arranged the piece of string on the tiles. But then the stick fell into the water.

"That man is completely bonkers," Kolt said. "I know he's supposed to be a genius, head of the Alexandrian library, teacher, poet, even an athlete—but how can a breakthrough in science be achieved with a stick and a piece of wobbly string?"

Then Eratosthenes started to panic.

"Girl!" he cried, turning to Gertie. "Can you help me, please—there isn't much time!"

"I can help you, master!" shouted the hairy man.

"No, it must be the child! She found the branch, it *must* be her."

Gertie jumped up and hurried past the furious-looking servant to the center of the house. It was burning hot in the midday sun, but Eratosthenes was determined to complete his experiment and asked Gertie to hold the stick steady in one place. Then he stared up into the blazing sunshine.

"You can go blind like that!" Kolt pointed out, his mouth full of spiced olives.

"Master, it is now precisely noon!" cried the hairy man.

Gertie watched as Eratosthenes carefully measured the stick's shadow with the string.

"7.2! 7.2!" Eratosthenes cried, jumping up. "You can let the stick go now, Gertie, we've done it—the angle of the stick's shadow is 7.2 degrees. And there's 360 degrees in a circle, and 7.2 goes into 360 exactly 50 times!"

"Which is good?" asked Gertie.

"My child, it's amazing, because right when we measured the shadow the stick made at noon, I know that 500 miles away in Syene, the sun was shining into a well, illuminating *only* the water, not the sides of the well, but just the water, so that there was *no* shadow. So if the world is 360 degrees, as any circle is, and the distance between my house and the well in Syene is 500 miles, then 7.2 times 50 equals 360 degrees, and 500 miles times 50 equals 25,000 miles, which must be the circumference of the world, in other words, the distance around the Earth from *here*," he said, pointing down at his left slipper, "to here!" he went on, pointing at the right.

Gertie wandered back over to Kolt and snapped a grape from the bunch. "That's nice," she said. "So you'll always know where your slippers are."

"Yes! Exactly, they can never be more than 25,000 miles away from each other."

Then he started dancing around.

"Praise the skies! May libations pour! It has been

achieved!" he cried, waving the stick and the piece of string in the air. "We've worked out how big the Earth is with a stick, string, and light."

"I stand corrected," Kolt said. "He's brilliant after all. I don't know where my slippers are, half the time."

18

Back to the Time Camels

Soon it was time to go.

"Well, I'm happy for you, Eratosthenes," Kolt said. "Seems like you've done something wonderful, but now that you've got your stick friend and your lucky string and are having fun with them, I think we'll be heading off back to the Time Ca—"

"Camel!" Gertie interrupted. "Time to get to our camel!"

"Yes, exactly." Kolt nodded. "Our time camels."

"But I've done it!" Eratosthenes insisted. "Thanks to you, I've accomplished the impossible, don't you see?"

He swept Kolt and Gertie into a hug and then launched into a mostly incoherent ramble, throwing his hands in the air and waving his stick around with so much excitement, the hairy man got whipped in the eye.

Gertie pretended to drop a grape, so no one could see her laughing.

"How lovely..." Kolt said, standing up. "How marvelous! String and shadows, what a brilliant game. I'm so happy for you, but we really must be going. Our camels need their camel food, and our tents have most likely blown away!"

Eratosthenes begged them to stay longer, but Kolt insisted and indicated to Gertie with his eyes that they should start moving toward the door.

"Take care of that eye!" Kolt called out to the hairy man, who was sitting down with a piece of camel cheese held over it.

Once outside, they walked away quickly down a cool, dark alley. Kolt seemed pleased.

"Well, that went rather well! You were excellent, Gertie, a proper Keeper if I ever saw one, well done, good thinking!"

"I'm not sure I understand how giving that man his pet stick is helping to save the human race."

"He needed that stick to measure how far around the Earth is, its circumference."

"But couldn't he have just used another stick?"

"The B.D.B.U. is never wrong about these things—and for reasons unknown to you or me, it was at that exact time under those exact conditions, with that plain-looking Persea branch that the mathematician was to conduct his experiment."

"For the good of humankind?"

"If the world can be sized, then it can be mapped and explored, and people can meet and swap ideas, and then new inventions can come, and people can grow and prosper."

"Who was that hairy man who answered the door?"

"The one who got whipped in the eye?" Kolt asked.

Gertie nodded. "I thought he was Eratosthenes's son, until he called him master."

"He was most likely a slave, Gertie. I'm sad to say this, but it was common practice in the ancient world for people to keep slaves."

"So the hairy man couldn't just leave if he wanted to?"

"No, slaves were bought and sold at markets. Let's hope Eratosthenes was a kind master."

"He shouldn't have been a master to begin with!"

"I agree with you," Kolt said. "But it takes a very special kind of genius to see the crimes that hide from us in plain sight."

Before leaving the city, Kolt stopped to pick up "essentials" they could eat on the way home, including a jar of honey with a distinctive smoky flavor, "though one has to be careful," he warned her, "not to end up with ancient honey from Corsica, which is poisonous."

Gertie was so full from the camels' milk cheese and olives that she couldn't even think of food, but she watched Kolt barter at the different market stalls, listening and looking for anything camel-like that might jog her memory of the word she'd heard herself say.

Despite the punishing heat, Gertie wished they could have stayed longer so that she might meet some children her age and find out if the Alexandrian nights were cool and pleasant to walk around in under the bright moon.

She wanted to learn what sort of games they played, what they dreamed about, things they had learned from living in the desert, and what they liked to drink and eat. Gertie sensed that, most of all, she wanted to make a friend.

"There's nothing like Alexandrian olives," Kolt remarked, as a shriveled woman (not unlike an olive herself) filled a cloth sack. "But this must still feel very strange for you."

It was beyond strange. Gertie wondered if her memory would ever come back, or if the only knowledge she would ever have of who she was would be from when she became a Keeper. Perhaps if she understood more, it might jog her old memory in some way.

"So returning things helps people learn, so they can live more and more peacefully together?"

"That's the basic idea, Gertie—education is a positive, guiding force in the world."

"I guess that makes sense, but then why are there so many wars? What if people use knowledge to control others?"

Kolt sighed. "That's along the lines of what the Losers believe. They think humans are not responsible enough to use knowledge wisely. But we Keepers believe the opposite, that with enough knowledge and education, people will eventually develop the wisdom they need for the good of all—don't forget our motto, *It could always be worse!*"

"But what does that mean?"

"That no matter what's going on—you must always keep hope alive in your heart."

"Who are these Losers anyway? Have you ever seen one?"

"Misguided misfits in my opinion," Kolt said hotly. "Their leader's name is Cava Calla Thrax. He was once a clever Roman Caesar disgusted by the brutal Roman way of life, who actually set out to do good...."

"What happened?"

"His ideas got twisted and he became quite ruthless. By trying to rid the world of darkness, he brought more into it. Then in his sixty-fourth year of life he completely disappeared, leaving only his books behind."

"He wrote books?"

"Yes, he was a scholar like Eratosthenes. The Losers formed about three thousand years later. They started as a group of bitter scientists obsessed with the work of Cava Calla Thrax, who had predicted that too much knowledge would be the downfall of human life, and that we should live in ignorance as neophobics—people who are afraid of anything new."

"But scientists? Don't they look for new things?"

"In theory, yes—but those that founded the Losers were consumed with anger."

"Why?"

"They had spent their entire working lives in an artificial intelligence lab trying to create a computer that would know everything."

"But they couldn't finish it?"

"Oh they finished it—but all it could do was make hot chocolate."

Gertie licked her lips. "And that's a bad thing?"

"The whole project became a joke. The scientists were the laughingstock of the world. Even the name of their computer, Vispoth, entered common usage as a word to describe something outrageously expensive and completely useless."

"Vispoth! That's the Losers' totally insane supercomputer!"

"Right, Gertie, so then the scientists stole it from the lab, went into hiding, and reprogrammed its memory with the complete works of Cava Calla Thrax, hoping it would tell them how to rid the world of knowledge and create widespread neophobia."

"Fear of new things."

"Exactly."

Gertie felt she was starting to understand.

"But that's not the worst bit. . . . One of the first things it spat out from its insane computer brain was that there was a 98.9 percent probability that beings from another dimension were aiding humanity by returning lost objects to the world."

"That's us, right?"

"So much for slipping through time unnoticed. . . ."

"But Kolt," Gertie asked curiously, "how do you know all this?"

"Mrs. Pumble cornered a Loser years ago during a mission and put truth spice in the moonberry juice he stole. We quickly found out that not only had our ancient order been discovered, but Vispoth was able to calculate when and where objects were most likely to be returned by Keepers of Lost Things."

"Is that how your key and time machine got stolen?"

Kolt nodded. "Vispoth knew which mission would take place in the Losers' natural lifetimes, and where in the world it would happen. So they flew down to South America, where they ambushed Mrs. Pumble and me in the rain forest as we were trying to return a beautiful set of panpipes."

Suddenly there was a loud *clonk*, as Kolt walked into something hard and metal.

"Finally!" he said. "I knew the Time Cat was around here somewhere."

Kolt uncloaked it and they both got inside.

"But to finish the story, Gertie—the stolen time machine and key were useless at first without the B.D.B.U. to decide the destination. However, when the Losers connected the key and box to Vispoth, it was somehow able to figure out the mechanics of time travel, create plans for a ship, and send Losers back to the Roman era, where they found their beloved author, Cava Calla Thrax, and whisked him away."

"That explains why he went missing suddenly from history."

"As if returning objects weren't dangerous enough—now Keepers were battling Losers for the fate of humankind. That's why you showing up was the best thing that's happened in centuries. You tipped the balance, Gertie—you're the new Keeper hope!"

Then Gertie had a thought. "But if the Losers started with books and a supercomputer, isn't that knowledge?"

"I know," Kolt chuckled. "But the irony is completely lost on them."

"Well, we're not going to let them win," Gertie said, her determination like a fire fed by everything she had learned. "And until I find my way home, I promise to help as much as I can."

As Kolt punched in the time codes, Gertie imagined human progress as brave people holding hands in a long line, passing ideas to one another—with the Losers trying to break that chain.

"Do we have to return through that battle?" Gertie asked, noticing a group of camel herders eyeing them with curiosity.

"Oh, goodness no, that was miles and miles away. Just press this...."

Kolt showed Gertie a white button with a smiling face drawn on it. "That's for home! I'll make one with your face too if you want."

When the camel herders decided to investigate the horseless green chariot, Kolt declared they had successfully done their duty, and it was probably time to get going. He took the time machine from the glove box, gave it to Gertie (who had Kolt's key ready), and pressed the button with the picture of his head on it.

There was a fizzing sensation, a series of light *pops,* and within a split second they had left the fabled ancient city of Alexandria and were rocketing over the graviton bridge in their old green car with dodgy locks and rust in the floor panels.

Unfortunately, on the final curve between the dimension of Earth and the Island of Skuldark, Kolt realized that one of the 101 automatic watches spinning under the hood had stopped working. Probably, he explained to Gertie (trying not to panic), on account of the cannon crown doing something to the balance-cap jewel, which in turn would have jammed the minute wheel and shredded the gluon exchange—resulting in a level 7 boomerang schlepp.

In other words, they were about to break down.

19

The Big Apple

IT ALL HAPPENED SO QUICKLY. The Time Cat began to sputter, then a weak tapping from the engine rose gradually to a series of bangs, then finally to a small explosion, which caused the old car to spin around, before a blinding flash of green light and a horrible thump, which meant they'd touched down.

"Oh dear, oh dear, oh heavens!" Kolt said, yanking off his seat belt. "Are you hurt, Gertie?"

"I'm fine, I think," she said, checking to see if all her limbs were where she remembered them. "But where are we?"

Peering out the windows, Gertie saw they had crash-landed in an enormous tree, with branches wide enough to walk on, and leaves the size of tablecloths.

"So this is how it feels to be a bug!" Gertie said, surprised at how calm she felt, considering that the Time Cat had almost exploded with her in it.

"Let's be very careful," Kolt warned her as they climbed out of the steaming car to check the damage. "We appear to be miles up from the ground in what I suspect is a dinosaur orchard."

"Dinosaurs?" Gertie asked. "I think I remember what they are. So we've gone even further back in time from the North African desert?"

"No, Gertie, forward! Way, way, way forward into the future. Look up!"

In the sky, Gertie saw thousands upon thousands of tiny dots darting about like dotty insects, zipping in all directions.

"What are they?"

"Space traffic," Kolt said. "Humans eventually left the Earth and moved into space just outside the atmosphere."

"But why?"

"Because six thousand years after Eratosthenes figured out how big the Earth was, it ended up being too small for everyone to live on comfortably. Population growth and the wear and tear of endless combustion, I'm afraid."

"Humans lived in space?"

"They did, Gertie. After a whole century of world conventions, committees, probes, prototypes, and three-course lunches, people moved into space, so Earth could be repaired and cultivated as a food planet with genetically modified semi-organic fruit trees that grow four miles high, blueberry bushes as tall as cliffs, and rice paddies producing rice grains the size of canoes."

"Maybe I'm from space. I never even thought about that."

"I'm not so sure, Gertie. You don't seem to know what anything is here. But let's get the Time Cat fixed as soon as possible, it was a lucky escape."

Once the engine had stopped smoking, Kolt fiddled with bushels of wires under the hood, as Gertie walked up and down the branch. Above her head dangled apples the size of boulders. Deep crimson with waxy skin that was so thick, she would have needed an ax to break through.

"I wish I could take a bite!"

Kolt looked up from what he was doing. "Imagine the pie we could make from just one! Though what I find most amazing is how the juiciness inside each apple is simply water that's traveled miles up from the ground through the roots."

Gertie stared past the giant leaves at all the colorful dots in the sky. Space people zipping about in their ships.

"Should we try to get help? From the people up there?"

"I'm afraid they already know we're here. It's forbidden to land in trees and go exploring dinosaur orchards without some kind of fruit permit," Kolt said. "So we really need to get going before we're arrested."

After assessing the damage, Kolt said they were going to need parts from the cottage.

Gertie volunteered.

"Go by yourself? You realize that if you don't come back I'll be stuck here?"

"Until you get snatched by the B.D.B.U."

"Very true, but in the meantime, anything could happen!"

"Of course I'll come back," Gertie said. "Just tell me how."

Kolt took a pocketknife from the Time Cat and cut a small piece of bark from the tree branch he was standing on. "Because we've broken down, and this is not a place the B.D.B.U. intended us to visit, the rules may be a little different."

Kolt handed Gertie the slice of tree bark.

"This is your ticket back," he said. "Once you arrive on Skuldark, it will be technically lost—and so because it's part of a living thing, and most living objects need immediate return, just make sure you're touching it, or it's in your pocket when you put the key in the time machine."

Then Kolt told Gertie the things he needed and where to find them.

"Oh! And you'd best bring a couple of seals, in case water gets in."

"Wow, okay . . . where would I find those? On the beach with Johnny the Guard Worm?"

Kolt was confused but then suddenly understood. "No, no, Gertie, not those kinds of seals. I need the ones in a drawer under the sink that's full of rubber rings to prevent leaks. And while you're at it, pick up a space-timing belt, and from a wooden box under the table marked DO NOT OPEN, I want you to bring a test tube of enriched seaweed powder, which should give the engine a boost, and get the watches spinning again.

"And don't hang about, Gertie! Don't go anywhere near

or even touch—or even breathe on—a magnet, and don't set your key down and walk away, and please don't get distracted by a Slug Lamp or something interesting on the kitchen table and forget about me."

Gertie watched his eyes dart about, scanning the tree branches above her head. "It's not the fruit police I'm worried about," he confessed. "It's the pollination drones."

Gertie promised to be extra careful as she retrieved the time machine from the glove box and inserted Kolt's key.

"It could always be worse!"

Almost instantly, Gertie found herself back in the kitchen of the Keepers' cottage, surprised by how still and dark it was. The fire had gone out, and the damp air smelled of wood smoke.

A few moments after her arrival, the nautical lamps flickered to life at the same time.

"Hello?" Gertie said. "Is someone here?"

It was strange to be alone again, even though Kolt's house was a place she felt safe enough to be herself, whoever that was.

She stared at her reflection in the mirror. Going back over all the things that had happened, she felt her feelings uncoil like an old spring.

"So you're Keeper of Lost Things," she said, and despite the mystery of who she was, and the hardships she had faced, something about those few words made the girl in the mirror smile.

"A Keeper," she said again, feeling something she hadn't felt before. A sort of pride, a confidence in what she now understood was a duty.

Halfway back to the kitchen was a tiny door with a sign that read BEDROOM 4.

As instructed, Gertie crouched and went in. It was more of a storage closet than a room, with almost every inch of space taken up by a huge glass tank, which Kolt had described as the sort of thing you'd normally see full of dangerous fish eyeballing you through the glass. But this one contained time itself, and was filled to the brim with thousands of wristwatches, pocket watches, calculator watches, water clocks, shadow clocks, maritime clocks (including the Harrison regulator), cosmic star threaders, space-time locators, and an ingenious timepiece, which gave the wearer electric shocks at every mealtime if he or she wasn't eating enough vegetables.

Gertie put her ear to the glass and listened to the delicate clicking of wheels and springs. The language of time. A framed letter hung beside the tank of watches.

> Dearest Kolt,
>   In answer to your question, I think time exists so that everything doesn't happen at once. Thanks again for finding my socks, and the bottle of moonberry juice.
> Onward!
> —Albert Einstein

At one end of the glass tank, there was a bright red button, and directly underneath an opening with a metal bucket to catch whatever came shooting through the hole. When Gertie pushed the button three times (as Kolt had instructed) there was a strange whirring noise, a rush of air, and three watches fell with a clunk into the bucket.

Strapping them on her arm, Gertie wondered who they belonged to, and how they had come to be lost in the first place.

After hurrying back to the kitchen, she scanned the wall of books, searching for the volume Kolt had asked for. She wondered if she would see that book written by Mrs. Pumble. According to what Kolt had said, she had found a way back to her family but, for some reason, had chosen to return to Skuldark. Gertie had so many questions she hoped the book might answer, but couldn't waste time looking for it now. She would ask Kolt where it was when she had completed her first mission as Keeper and they were lounging comfortably by the fire, their mouths fizzing with moonberry juice.

Many of the books in the tall case were in languages that Gertie couldn't understand—though some of the titles she could read seemed quite interesting:

The Explosive Power of Spices

The Riddle of Teeth

A Poisoner's Companion

The Bovine Divine:
A History of Supernatural Cows

As Gertie scanned the shelves, one volume began to glow. Then to her surprise, it began sliding out of its place, and would have fallen to the floor had Gertie not lunged to catch it in midair. She suspected it was the book Kolt had asked her to get, but it turned out to be something completely different, an illustrated manual of some kind:

Caring for Your Robot Rabbit Boy:
A Complete Guide to the Series 7

It had to be the work of the B.D.B.U., Gertie thought, and she tucked it into her cloak. Then she saw the book Kolt had requested:

The Dangerous History of Attraction:
Why Magnets Matter

She grabbed it and went over to the food cupboard to search for the block of chocolate marmalade cake Kolt wanted.

"Just look for an expiration date in 1834," he'd said, "and you'll know you have the right one."

Then she fetched the seals, space-timing belt, and vial of super-seaweed powder from the box marked DO NOT OPEN (which she opened).

Although Kolt had assured Gertie that the time machine would work anywhere, she took it outside along with the books, cake, spare parts, and three timepieces on her arm, to the faded patch of yellow grass where the Time Cat was usually parked. It had stopped raining, but the ground was soggy, and her sandals were soon soaked. It was hard to believe that only hours ago, she'd been dying of heat and thirst in the African desert. She checked to make sure the dinosaur apple tree bark was in her pocket and then fed her key into the box.

With a pleasant buzzing and a loud pop, Gertie was returned to the branch where they had broken down. Kolt was standing in the same position, with exactly the same look of fear on his face.

"Brilliant, you were only gone nine minutes!"

He took from Gertie everything he had asked for, and began to hammer at something in the engine. Gertie sat down with the book she had brought on Robot Rabbit Children.

After a while, Kolt appeared from under the hood with splashes of oil and green slime on his face.

"It should work now. I only needed two timepieces in the end; keep the third and toss it back in the time tank when we get home."

"Maybe I could return it?" Gertie said hopefully, looking at the small gold watch with plain black numbers. "It could be my next mission as Keeper?"

Kolt tore some cake from the loaf Gertie had brought.

"I'm afraid not," he said, chewing around the words. "We can only return what the B.D.B.U. instructs us to, not the things we wish."

"Oh yes, I forgot," she said, blushing.

Then suddenly, the watch on her wrist began to glow.

Gertie jumped to her feet. "Does that mean we can return it?"

Kolt was surprised. "The B.D.B.U. must think you're ready for your first solo mission."

"Solo mission?" Gertie said. "So I get to drive the Time Cat by myself?"

Kolt laughed nervously. "Well, no, not exactly, I'll come with you, but you can make all the decisions."

Gertie put the time machine back in the glove box, and they strapped themselves in. Kolt said he was relieved the orchard police hadn't shown up—or worse, one of the gigantic insect drones.

Suddenly, a heavy, teeth-rattling vibration passed through the cabin of the Time Cat.

"Oh dear," he said. "Maybe I spoke too soon."

"Are we breaking down again?"

"No," Kolt replied with an edge in his voice. "I haven't even turned the engine on yet. That's something else entirely, something outside."

Gertie scanned the skies. "A bee drone?"

"Let's not find out!"

At first, the Time Cat's motor wouldn't start and just

"What was that?" asked Gertie.

Kolt fiddled with some wires under the steering wheel. Then with a choking sound (as though the motor was simply clearing its throat) the Time Cat began to chug. Kolt pressed the Home button, and the old car fizzed and shuddered, but then a moment before they hit the graviton bridge the dark shadow swooped down, so that it hovered just a few feet over the Time Cat's hood. Kolt slammed on the brakes. It was not a bee drone or the orchard police but an enormous, thrumming spaceship in the shape of a giant, battered doll head.

Kolt gasped. "Losers!"

"What? Who?" Gertie said, trying to make sense of what she was seeing.

"It's Doll Head! The Losers' patrol ship."

"What should we do?" Gertie said, sensing something dreadful about to happen.

Kolt frantically pushed buttons and pulled levers, as the dashboard blazed red with warning lights. "They're trying to hitch a ride to Skuldark across the graviton bridge. We're going to have to make a run for it!"

20

Doll Head

"THIS IS THE ONLY WAY!" Kolt yelled, as the Time Cat rolled sideways off the branch and began hurtling toward the ground at an unthinkable speed. "If we went back to Skuldark now, they might follow us!"

Giant tree leaves slapped the window as Kolt fought to regain control. Gertie was pinned back in her seat by the sheer force of their dive.

"Let's hope the emergency rockets heat up in time."

"Or what will happen?"

"We'll hit the ground, Gertie, or get ripped in two by a branch, *then* hit the ground."

Doll Head was right behind them. Gertie could see the sinister face in the Time Cat's only side mirror. The head was dirty and old, like something from a nightmare rather than a toy cupboard. Its mouth was locked in a grin of black and grimy teeth, while glass eyes stared freakishly at its intended victims—in this case, Gertie and Kolt.

"Why are they are in a giant, weird doll head?"

"Because Losers take pleasure in spreading fear," Kolt explained. "People can't learn anything when they're afraid, you see. And there's nothing creepier than a hairless doll with tooth decay."

"Except . . ." Gertie said without thinking, "an arm playing tennis with a chopped-off hand!"

"Wonderful!" Kolt laughed. "Only a true Keeper would make jokes as we're tumbling to our deaths."

"What about the emergency rockets?"

Kolt looked at the dial. "Warm, but still not hot."

Doll Head was closing in, dodging leaves, trying to get right up behind them as Kolt did his best to steer around giant pieces of fruit.

"I just don't get it. If the Losers hate technology, why are they flying around in a giant doll-head spaceship?"

"Because like most maniacs, their own rules don't apply to themselves!"

As another dinosaur apple loomed dead ahead, Gertie banged her fist against the emergency rockets' dial.

Kolt scowled. "I'm sure that won't wooooooorrrrkkk!"

The Time Cat was rocked by four enormous bangs, followed by the sound of glass shattering, as fizzing corks exploded through the broken lights into the smug face of Doll Head.

"There go the rare Jaguar taillights," Kolt cried. "But at least we have rocket power."

Gertie looked back and saw yellow mist engulfing their pursuer.

"What's all that smoke?"

"It's not smoke." Kolt laughed. "It's champagne. Each taillight contains three bottles of vintage French wine, which, in the event of an emergency free-fall, can be heated to 604 degrees Fahrenheit and then released through metal straws giving us jet propulsion for about ten minutes."

"Then what?"

"We have to wait until we're back in the 1820s to sneak into Louis XVIII's wine cellar at Versailles to borrow a few more bottles."

"No, I mean after the jet power runs out."

"Oh, we crash, unless we find somewhere to land first."

"Then let's start looking!"

Kolt pulled back firmly on the steering wheel, and the Time Cat's hood began to rise. They were no longer falling but blasting through the dinosaur orchard so quickly it was a miracle they didn't smack into any low-hanging fruit.

"We've lost them!" Kolt said triumphantly. "One of the champagne corks must have hit Doll Head in the eye. Oh, I'd love to have seen the looks on their faces."

Kolt slowed down and circled a few times to make sure there was no sign of their pursuer.

"What would happen if we got caught?"

"They would force us to take them back to Skuldark,

because it's the B.D.B.U. they really want. Without that, our Keeper way of life would be finished."

"Would they kill us?" Gertie said with a gulp.

"They'd probably try to get us on their side first, but Vispoth is unpredictable, and who knows what it would tell Thrax to order."

Gertie glanced nervously in her mirror.

"Don't worry, Gertie! Johnny the Guard Worm is our first line of defense."

"But there's only two of us left."

"I'm afraid so. There used to be many more, like I told you, all living on Skuldark. It's truly a mystery what happened. I mean—where could they all have gotten to?"

"I bet the Losers have something to do with it!"

When the champagne began to fizzle out, Kolt said the Time Cat would have to land immediately, and they descended slowly in search of a place to set down.

The whipping leaves of dinosaur apple trees soon gave way to ruined buildings, windowless skyscrapers, and advertisements too sun-faded to read.

"I don't believe it!" Gertie cried, craning to see out of the Time Cat's dirty windows. "I know where we are!"

21

The Abandoned City

"I KNOW WHAT THESE THINGS ARE CALLED!" Gertie exclaimed, pointing to something in the distance. "They're billboards! And that one is for barbeque macaroni and cheese. I don't have any memory of eating it, but my mouth is watering so I must have liked it, right?"

"Maybe," Kolt said. "Can't say I've ever eaten any myself."

They swooped down between gray towers grown over with vines. "Do you know where we are? Do people live here, Kolt?"

"We're on Earth, but no one has lived in this city for hundreds and hundreds of years."

"Then maybe it's where I *used* to live."

They located a bare strip of road that was mostly grown over with weeds, and Kolt brought the Time Cat down with a bump.

"Can we *please* get out and explore? I think I may start to remember things!"

"Well, we really must return to Skuldark, now that we've lost Doll Head. We're technically not supposed to be here."

"Please, Kolt, this could be my chance to find home."

"Oh all right," he sighed. "I suppose it can't hurt. Twenty minutes and not a second more."

Gertie leaned over and gave him a quick hug, then rushed outside. Kolt got out too.

"The city is Los Angeles!" he called after her, stepping cautiously over the cracked tarmac. "Centuries after the evacuation."

"What's an evacuation?"

"People leaving in a hurry."

"Where did they go?"

"Up! Gertie, remember? As I mentioned, it had already been decided that the planet would be turned into a garden for food—but as humans were preparing to leave for their floating communities just outside the Earth's atmosphere, something happened that made them scramble to leave sooner."

"What happened? An explosion? A giant earthquake?"

"I'd rather not say just now," Kolt said, looking around nervously. "Let's hope the last few centuries fixed the problem."

Gertie couldn't believe what was happening. It was like a dream within a dream. She recognized almost everything, from taxicabs abandoned with their yellow doors rusted open to the shells of hot dog carts full of colorful nesting birds. She felt like if she turned the right corner, she might run straight into her family, or least something that would make her remember them.

"It's amazing," Gertie said, searching around inside herself for an actual memory, "like I know what to do here." She turned to Kolt. "Like I could live here!"

"Well, it's abandoned, Gertie—no one has lived here for a very long time. Perhaps if we're ever sent back by the B.D.B.U. when it's inhabited, you'll really have a chance to find home."

"Could that happen?"

"It could, but we might hope it doesn't. Long before the evacuation, Los Angeles was the most dangerous city to live in because of the Information War."

"I don't remember anything about being in a war."

Kolt bent down and picked something up. Gertie watched him brush the dust off. It was a plastic card with a photo and bar code.

"It's a knowledge license," he said, "also known as a brain card." He passed it to Gertie. "Seem familiar?"

She looked at the young woman in the photograph, smiling as though to disguise the terrible things that might have happened to make brain cards a part of everyday life.

"What were they for?"

"After the Information War, it was decided that you could only share information if it was factual, or based on firsthand experience—this was to stop opinions and feelings being passed off as facts, which caused chaos, especially in the medical field. Anyone posting false or misleading information would lose their brain card and be limited to 'live speech' for two years."

"Did it work?"

"I don't know. . . . I've found books on dinosaur-tree farming, and adjusting to life in space, but never anything on the aftermath of the brain-card experiment—which might mean it didn't work. Plus, Gertie, this is the first time I've ever seen North America since the evacuation."

Gertie understood why. "Because if there's no one here— there can be nothing to return."

"That is correct."

"But you've taken things to people in space?"

"You'll find oxygen suits are in a sealed cupboard at the back of the Sock Drawer."

With only ten minutes left to explore, Gertie was desperate to remember something concrete about her life that she could take back to Skuldark.

"Please be careful!" Kolt called out, as she went from building to building, looking inside—even rattling the handles of doors to see if anything was open.

Every block or so, a giant tree stump rose out of the ruins and soared high above them. The old city was cool and dry as the dinosaur leaves and branches blocked direct sun.

"*Please* be careful," Kolt said again. "I'm not sure if we're alone down here!"

"People got left behind?"

"Not people, Gertie—not humans."

"I don't feel afraid at all," Gertie admitted. "I've waited too long to feel this way. I know all the names for things," she said, pointing. "Those are parking meters, and that funny circle over there is where you chain up a bicycle."

"But can you feel your memory actually coming back?"

"No, not really," Gertie admitted with some disappointment. "And there *are* things here I don't know," she said, going over to a glass dome with nothing inside but a comfortable-looking pink chair.

"That's a Boon Bubble," Kolt explained. "Back when Los Angeles was inhabited, if someone on the street felt ill, or couldn't breathe, or had a pain in their chest, they could go inside the Boon Bubble, sit in the chair, and get immediate medical treatment. Tiny computers in the glass would scan the body and release medicine in the form of a spray while the chair gave you a massage and played smooth jazz."

Gertie rubbed away the dust and looked in.

"I don't remember it," she said sadly.

Colorful shapes in the distance turned out to be an old playground. With only five minutes left, Gertie amused herself by swinging on the monkey bars and spinning around on a giant wheel that you could stand on. "Anything else spring to mind?" Kolt called out as she revolved.

"Not really," replied Gertie, running toward some swings. "But I love these!"

"Well, sorry to rush you, but Doll Head might be up

there searching for us. And we have a new mission to complete."

Gertie glanced at the gold watch on her wrist. It was still glowing.

"If the B.D.B.U. has decided this little watch is important to the human race," Gertie said, jumping off the swing, "then let's go."

Kolt held up his small wooden box and Keeper's key. "Remember to . . ."

"Yes, yes, always take the time machine and key with you when you leave the Time Cat. And no magnets!"

Then something occurred to her. "You don't think the Losers know about me, do you? And that's why they followed us?"

"No, why would you say that? How could they?"

"I don't know. . . . I just thought of it, that's all."

Kolt stared with a suspicious look that caught her by surprise.

"What?"

"Oh, nothing," he said. "Nothing at all."

When they were halfway back to the Time Cat, Kolt stopped walking suddenly.

"Don't move!" he whispered. "Don't move an inch!"

Gertie froze.

"We're being watched," he said. "There's something over to your right . . . the building behind the rusty shopping carts."

Gertie slowly turned to look. It was a warehouse of some kind, with crumbling walls and green plants growing in the cracks. Attached to the front of the building was an old sign that read:

NEW HOLLYWOOD TOYS & GIFTS
WE HAVE A SURPRISE FOR YOU!

Inside each enormous, rusty letter, Gertie could see movement: what looked like small creatures shuffling about inside the hollow metal words.

"What are they?"

"For goodness' sake, don't move, Gertie. We're in deep trouble now. They're robot pet children."

"What's so scary about that?"

"It's why people abandoned Earth early!"

"Are they dangerous?"

"Yes they are! So try not to show any kind of emotion whatsoever, and let's get out of here."

"But where did they come from?" Gertie whispered.

"There was a time," Kolt said, "when people didn't want the trouble of raising real children anymore, but craved more than just a pet. So a computer genius, who also happened to be a veterinary surgeon who also happened to be a child psychologist, invented a creature that was part robot, part animal, part child, who could talk, dance, sing, read, write, even do yoga—a little friend who was capable of deep feelings, but who never expected you to pick up its drop-pings because it didn't do any."

The Time Cat was now in view.

"C'mon, Gertie, almost there, but no sudden move-ments, and definitely no smiling—the last thing we need is another chase."

Gertie just couldn't understand why the creatures were so dangerous. "Did they attack their owners or something?" she said, tiptoeing behind Kolt. "Were they vicious?"

"No, nothing like that. They were very popular at first, but then people got bored looking after them, and wanted to be free. The stores refused to take them back, not having the facilities to look after the poor creatures once they were switched on, and so people abandoned them in the streets, or drove them out to the woods, or to the tops of mountains."

Gertie was horrified. "That's so mean!"

"Careful, Gertie! Don't start feeling sorry for them—they're programmed to detect a sympathetic heart within two square miles."

"So what happened?"

"The mad genius who invented them was furious when the goverment demanded that she reprogram each robot animal child to be less needy of love and more capable of washing floors, scrubbing toilets, and vacuuming up crumbs. By this time she was the richest woman in the world, but had also gone insane. She rounded up every single aban-doned robot pet device, made them self-powering, virtually indestructible, and with the means to defend themselves against abusive owners. Then she released every single unit back into society."

"Without an Off switch?"

"It was madness! The day she opened the doors of the factory, millions of them walked out into the sunshine, more desperate than ever for hugs, kisses, attention, stories, lullabies, even birthday parties. They could never be switched off, and they never aged. This new breed, their inventor called the Forever Friend."

"And that's why humans left planet Earth in such a hurry? To get away from their Forever Friends?"

Kolt grinned. "A case of *cuteness overloadus* if you ask me."

When they were only a few yards from the Time Cat, there was a clanking of metal parts.

"Oh no!" Kolt said, as they both turned around. One of the robot animal pets had caught up with them. It appeared to be some kind of grimy rabbit with the ability to stand on its back legs and walk upright.

"Shoo!" Kolt hissed. "Go away!"

"Wait!" Gertie said. "That's a Robot Rabbit Boy Series 7! Just like in the book I found at the cottage!"

"What book?"

Gertie bent down and smiled. "Hey there!" she said, reaching out her hand. The Series 7 rabbit had a round metal belly but genuine rabbit face, ears, and soft paws, which trembled with excitement from the very likely possibility that, after hundreds of years alone in an abandoned city, it might finally get a hug.

"We *must* go, Gertie," Kolt insisted. "There's no room for hitchhikers."

"But look at its cute glowing eyes!" she said, shuffling toward it. "We can't just leave him here. He likes us."

"For goodness' sake, look around!"

From every rooftop, window, hole in the ground, and even the rusted-out sockets of car headlights, they were being watched. Not only watched—but studied, examined, and scrutinized by an army of forgotten robot beavers, gerbils, kittens, puppies, squirrels, koala bears, wolf cubs, owls, pigeons, guinea pigs, and piglets. Gertie even noticed robot hamster babies still waiting for their aluminum foil diapers to be changed.

"Be careful!" Kolt warned Gertie. "They're programmed to recognize love. Show any sign of affection and we're done for!"

But it was too late. Gertie already felt herself getting attached to the Series 7 who was himself mesmerized by the glowing fondness in her eyes. The legion of lonely pets sensed Gertie's desire to start hugging, and were now scrambling toward her, their fluffy circuits blazing with love.

Gertie and Kolt bolted for the Time Cat as the army of fur and steel bore down upon them.

"Bye!" Gertie cried out to the rabbit creature through the side window. "Hope we meet again someday!"

"Come on! Come on!" Kolt screamed, pumping the gas pedal. The old motor roared to life as they popped, fizzed, and in a flash of silver light appeared suddenly on a dismal city street surrounded by horses, trams, and strange-looking cars that were chugging along at walking speed.

"What happened?" Gertie said. "Where are we?"

Kolt pointed to the glowing watch on Gertie's wrist. "I didn't have time to push the Home button, so the B.D.B.U. must have sent us to where we have to return the watch."

"Well, where's that?" Gertie said, looking around for a clue.

Just then, a piece of newspaper conveniently blew across the crowded street and onto the windshield of the Time Cat. Kolt leaned forward.

"We're in London!" he said. "October 6th, 1927."

Gertie read the headline that was below the date in big letters.

Bravest Woman in the World, Mercedes Gleitze, to Swim Across English Channel—Despite Losing Lucky Gold Watch

22

The Frozen Mascot

GERTIE HELD UP HER WRIST. "This must be the lucky watch! Look, it's the same one as in the picture."

Kolt opened his window to grab the leaf of newsprint. "What a stroke of luck!"

"So we're in London," Gertie said, looking around at the men in dark suits and women in tall feathery hats. "Have you been here? Where is it?"

"It's in far western Europe, capital city of an island that's known for bad weather, horrible food, and people who are exceedingly polite—when they're not trying to invade your country."

Kolt pushed a button, and the engine turned over with a groan.

"We can't stay in the middle of the road," he said. "Let's find somewhere to park."

"But is there a way we can get back to that abandoned city?" Gertie asked. "I felt closer to my family and my old life there than anywhere else so far."

Kolt said nothing and steered the Time Cat down a narrow street, parking between two shops, Turnbull & Asser Shirtmakers and Bates Hats.

"Kolt!" Gertie said, irritated by his refusal to answer.

"I know it must be frustrating," he replied gently, "but for now we have a watch to return—and it's your first mission, so let's just do our best, and talk about everything else later, when we can write things down and start keeping a record."

Gertie adjusted the pretty gold timepiece on her wrist. "You're right," she said. "I wanted to return it, and the B.D.B.U. let me, so I'd better focus on what I'm doing."

Across Jermyn Street was a shop window full of socks, umbrellas, cravats, ties, pajama sets, silver straws for making fizzy drinks less fizzy, evening gloves, driving gloves, dinner gloves, fingerless gloves, even gloveless fingers for eating oysters. In other words, Kolt said, necessities, luxuries, and niceties that most people in history never dreamed they would need (and probably never would).

Behind them, men with aprons tied over starched, collarless shirts and black trousers were unloading barrels of ale from a delivery truck. Gertie watched as they barked instructions to one another and then rolled the barrels down wooden planks into a basement. Someone else was up on a ladder, dusting the restaurant sign that had a drawing of a friendly lobster in a top hat.

"That's odd," Gertie said. "If I were a lobster, I definitely wouldn't be trying to get people into a restaurant that *served* lobster—I'd be trying my best to look poisonous."

There were fewer people on this street, and most were carrying small boxes rolled in brown paper and tied with string.

"So what now?" Gertie said, looking at their ancient North African costumes. "How are we supposed to blend in?"

"See what I mean about the B.D.B.U.?" Kolt grumbled. "Any normal book—even your basic encyclopedia, even a comic—would have brought us home so we could change in the Sock Drawer. We don't even have money. We might starve on this mission!"

Gertie read the front page of the newspaper that Kolt had grabbed from the windshield.

"Kolt, look! It says the swimmer who is missing her watch is getting an award at a place called the Ritz Hotel tonight during something called a masquerade ball."

"That's a costume party," Kolt said. "Maybe we'll go unnoticed after all?"

Gertie felt triumphant, as though everything were part of a perfect plan. "So us coming straight here was exactly what the the B.D.B.U. wanted!"

"Are you sticking up for the old book?"

Just then, a bell rang loudly somewhere along the street, and a young man exited a shop dressed as a clown.

Gertie and Kolt, thinking the same thing, jumped out of the Time Cat as the man bounded toward them along the sidewalk in oversize red shoes.

"Whoa!" he said with a broad American accent. "How terrific you both look!" Then he pointed to the Time Cat. "And what a spiffy automobile. I love the rabbit emblem on the bumper!"

Gertie and Kolt turned sharply to see Robot Rabbit Boy, frozen solid to the rear bumper of the Time Cat.

"Oh dear," Kolt muttered. "He must have followed us."

"Well, we can't leave him here," Gertie said, trying to hide her excitement. "The poor thing is frozen stiff."

"We'll have to deal with it later, Gertie," Kolt said, in hushed tones so the man in the clown suit wouldn't hear. "We have more important Keeper business to attend to."

The friendly American clown kept saying how beautiful the Time Cat was. "I'll bet it's a lovely car to drive."

"Oh yes," said Kolt, "she really flies!"

"Shame about the broken taillights," the man pointed out. "An accident, I'm guessing? Other drivers can be such losers."

Kolt nodded with delight. "That's exactly what they are!"

While Kolt chatted with the friendly clown, Gertie knelt down and winked at the Series 7 Forever Friend that— despite being completely frozen—managed to shake an icy, worn-out rabbit paw in greeting.

"We have to go now," Gertie whispered, "but I know the perfect place for you to sleep back at the cottage after you've had a nice bath."

Robot Rabbit Boy tried to nod, but the ice encasing his neck was too thick, so instead he twitched one droopy ear.

"Say . . ." Kolt said to the clown, "it seems like we're on our way to the same costume party. How about we go together?"

"Suits me," said the clown.

Kolt was pleased with their good fortune. "A costume party!" he said in a fake British accent. "A bloomin' costume party! Yes please, I do think so, jolly good. . . ."

Together, the trio walked toward a glowing sign with the words RITZ HOTEL spelled out in tiny light bulbs.

"Oh dear," Kolt said, biting his lip, "this might be quite fancy."

"Just say we're ancient shepherds from the sand dunes of North Africa," suggested Gertie, "but maybe hold off on the fake British accent."

They followed the friendly clown up some marble steps and stood beneath a blue awning, beside a revolving door.

"My name is Fred," said the clown, "and I'm visiting from New York."

They watched as he fished out two paper tickets from his pocket and presented them to Gertie.

"I'm acting in a musical comedy," he said. "It's called *Lady, Be Good!* and it's my first big European show. Take these tickets for tomorrow night. In case you're free, it's really a hoot—you'll laugh your heads clean off!"

"That would be very nice," Gertie said, taking them. "Thank you." She knew they would be long gone by then, but didn't want to hurt the young man's feelings.

"You two seem like a swell pair!" The man grinned. "If you want to meet after the show, just hang around when the curtain falls, and if anyone asks, tell them you're waiting for Fred Astaire, that's me."

"Thanks, Fred," Gertie said. "Good luck with it, and thanks for being so nice to us."

Then with a smile and a little dance, the young American ushered Gertie and Kolt into the lobby of the Ritz Hotel.

"What a lovely man," Kolt said. "I hope he makes it as an actor, I really do."

The Palm Court was overflowing with jesters, princesses, kings, peasants, wizards, queens, angels, someone dressed as a toothbrush, devils, dragons, giant fish, and even a knight in armor whose helmet had gotten stuck, and who was surrounded by waiters whittling away with can openers. Gertie knew that somewhere in the chaos of the costume party was a young woman missing a watch. All she had to do was find her.

23

Kolt Disappears

WHEN THEY GOT TO THE BALLROOM, Fred melted into the crowd. Gertie was glad to see that everyone around them (except for the waiters in double-breasted white jackets with silver trays) was decked out in strange costumes. It made her and Kolt seem normal and not two time travelers from an ancient order of Keepers, responsible for the fate of humankind.

A jazz band was in full swing. People were dancing madly, throwing their heads back with laughter and kicking their heels in the air. Soon, Gertie was so swept up in the excitement that she nearly forgot why she was there.

"The watch!" she told herself. "Focus on the watch."

The air in the ballroom was thick with cigarette smoke, and it was hard to breathe. After sampling a few of the delicious things being carried around on silver trays, Kolt motioned for Gertie to follow him out a side door. They found themselves in a well-lit corridor of thick carpet, where there were rows and rows of doors with brass numbers on them.

"What's with all the smoking?" Gertie said.

"It's the 1920s! People had no idea it was bad for you."

Gertie held up her arm with the watch on it. "How are we ever going to find the person this watch belongs to with all these people dancing and screaming?"

Kolt didn't seem at all fussed. "Dealing with chaos is part of a Keeper's job," he said. "You must learn to act and think quickly!"

"Right," Gertie said, remembering the Keeper's motto. "It could always be worse, I suppose."

"Yes, it could, very much so."

Gertie brought the watch to her ear and listened to the purr of springs and wheels inside the golden case. "It's not glowing anymore," she said. "What does that mean?"

"It doesn't have to glow all the time. Just imagine we're in an ocean of fish," Kolt said. "You have to move with the current. Remember that the item *wants* to be found and will glow or heat up, or even vibrate when you get close to the target."

"So I'll just move with the current?"

"Yes, Gertie, glide in the stream, but stay alert. You'll find clues if you look for them."

Three waiters rushed past with an enormous bouquet of fruit set in ice.

"I didn't think it would be this hard to find the woman,

Mercedes what's-her-name," Gertie said, looking at her wrist. "It's just a little watch."

"Mercedes Gleitze," Kolt reminded her. "And this is your first solo mission." He smiled. "So just do your best."

A pair of men in overalls and thick gloves grunted under the weight of an ice swan balanced on their shoulders. Then another man rushed forward to open the ballroom door.

"Ladies and gentlemen," came an amplified voice from inside, "may I present to you Great Britain's first ever female swimming champion, who will attempt a cross-Channel paddle from France to England tomorrow before dawn . . . introducing the marvelous and daring Miss Mercedes Gleitze!"

"That must be her!" Gertie cried, her voice drowned out by the applause. The watch was glowing violet, and had begun to pulse.

Kolt bolted through the doors into the ballroom, but, when Gertie tried to follow, a man in a gray pinstripe suit with shiny hair blocked her path.

"And where is it, mademoiselle, that you think you are going?" said the maître d'hôtel. He glared at Gertie, smoothing the ends of a thin moustache.

For a second, Gertie was tempted to just tell the truth. She imagined herself explaining that she had traveled through time from a magical island over a graviton bridge through a dinosaur orchard, via an abandoned city of the future full of robot pets and brain cards, with a man who was a hundred years old, or maybe two hundred.

The other option was to simply push past him. It might have worked—or at least caused enough of a scene to get Kolt's attention—but the door had already swung closed.

Gertie pointed in the direction of the ballroom, where, at that moment, on stage, stood the champion swimmer to whom the timepiece belonged. "But sir, I have to see the woman in there. We have important business."

"Believe me, we would all like an audience with the daring Mademoiselle Gleitze, but the Ritz Ballroom is not the place for young ladies, even polite ones such as yourself."

"But!" Gertie protested, "I have to—"

"No buts, *please* no buts, I *'ate* buts," the man insisted. "You must come with me, *ma petite fille.*"

Gertie was going to shout for Kolt but knew he wouldn't have heard above the din of cheering that now filled the ballroom.

When the man motioned for a waitress to assist in the capture of "a lost child," Gertie had little choice but to be escorted down the long corridor.

Pushing through some double doors, they passed through the kitchen, where men and women with tall white hats stood on ladders over enormous metal pots with boat oars. There was so much steam in some places that Gertie considered trying to escape. If she could make it outside, back to the Time Cat, she knew Kolt would find her eventually. Robot Rabbit Boy was there too—probably still frozen to the bumper.

"We are now entering the *'all* of desserts," the man said, "You must be quiet—step in silence, mademoiselle, for the most dazzling cakes in *ze 'ole* world are in the final stages of beautification."

Despite her frustration, Gertie marveled as whole teams of skilled workers bent over enormous, revolving ceramic bowls of colored mixtures. Others were laying tablecloths of yellow marzipan over mountains of fruitcake.

A master pâtissier patrolled the room with a magnifying glass and spoon, stopping from time to time for mouthfuls and then spitting into a bright pink handkerchief with either a word of praise or something vulgar that made the waitress cover her ears. In the background, one of the cooks was playing a delicate stringed instrument that was as tall as a person and twice as heavy.

"Music is the secret. . . ." The man winked at Gertie. "You must keep fruit in a trance so it doesn't get scared and go sour."

Gertie looked at the waitress and whispered, "I never knew blueberries had feelings?"

The waitress nodded. "It's one of the hotel's many secrets."

When they entered a narrow white passage with wooden planks for a floor, they stopped beside a rack of heavy coats. The waitress took one down from a brass hook and helped Gertie get into it.

"Cold storage," the man explained, putting on a tiny gingham moustache scarf.

Through the freezing air they marched past giant blocks

of ice with teams of men and women chipping them into different animals.

At the end of the frosty chamber, they stepped through a heavy white door that was frozen on the inside with a thick layer of clear ice. Outside was another set of brass hooks. After hanging their coats up, the man pushed a fat button on a wall and a door opened.

"We have now arrived at the correct elevator for mademoiselle."

He smiled and ushered Gertie toward it, but she stood there not moving, with the sense that something horrible was about to happen. She turned and looked for somewhere to run, but was blocked on all sides.

Finally the waitress took Gertie's arm and forcefully led her inside. "C'mon, miss, it's down to the basement for you."

24

The Girl Who Loves Bones

When the elevator doors opened, Gertie got a great surprise.

It wasn't a pit of bubbling mud into which she would be dangled, or a spiral-eyed snake with an appetite for girls with bad memories. In fact, it wasn't anything scary at all, but a party—the wildest most chaotic scene Gertie had ever witnessed, and attended only by children. If the celebration upstairs in the Palm Court had seemed crazy, then this other party now taking place made the grown-ups look as if they had been asleep.

This party was what every party in the history of parties had tried to be.

Gertie's jaw dropped. Not only were there ice animals with cakes and plums and chocolates balanced on their frozen bodies, but *real* animals. Two live giraffes towered over the madness, leaning their long necks down to lick the smaller iced versions of themselves. Three small children had found a way to scramble onto the animals' backs and were balanced dangerously, holding on for their lives by a few sticky strands of giraffe hair. Gertie had never seen anything like it—or at least anything she could remember seeing.

There was even a trapeze, and one tiny girl swung wildly over everyone's heads.

"Wheeeeeeeeeeeeeeee!" she cried. "Wheeeeeeeeeeeee."

It was out of control, and a miracle no one had been killed—or at least sat on by an elephant that was picking up apples from the fruit platter and firing them mean-spiritedly at people's heads.

Everyone was in some kind of costume, and so Gertie passed unnoticed as she stepped from the small elevator through the swarms of children eating, singing, running, and dancing to the live jazz band—which itself was made up of children in tuxedos with carnation flowers in their jacket lapels.

Gertie felt so drawn in by the fun going on around her that, for a few moments, she again forgot all about the watch she'd come to return. She wondered if this wasn't the place and time she had been lost from—perhaps these children were all her friends?

Without thinking, Gertie began to shake her arms, then her legs, and before she knew it, she was dancing along with everyone else at the party. A girl standing nearby noticed Gertie and came over.

"Who are *you*?" she shouted above the blasting trumpets and saxophones. She had short black hair with a fringe, a wide face, and freckles on each cheek.

"Er, Gertie Milk . . . I think!"

The girl grabbed Gertie's arm and swung her toward a small group of dancing children.

"This is Gertrude Milk!" she announced. "My new friend!"

The girls turned and stared at Gertie for a moment, then went back to shaking their heads and throwing up their gloved hands in time to a frenzied clarinet solo.

The girl with black hair said her name was Miss Mary Leakey. Gertie sensed that Mary was just a little older than her.

After demonstrating a few dance steps, Mary leaned in and said, in a loud voice, "We're flappers, don't you know? That's why our hair is bobbed like this. Are you a flapper too?"

"I don't really know what I am," Gertie said. "It's sort of a long story. I feel like I could be anything, but I am so happy to meet another girl!"

Mary took Gertie's hand and led her to a quieter part of the ballroom, next to a table laid out with every kind of food imaginable.

"I simply love your costume," Mary said. Then she looked closely at the birthmark on Gertie's face. "How interesting. Is that makeup for the party, or is it a real birthmark?"

"It's real," Gertie said. "It's me."

"If people stare at you," Mary smiled, "it's probably

because they're simply not used to seeing a birthmark. People will always be interested in things that are not common, which is something you can use to your advantage."

Gertie decided that she liked Mary very much.

"It's nice you're so honest," Gertie said. "I mean that you know yourself well enough to say things."

"People tell me I'm confident, but I think it's my scientific brain. My big dream is to go exploring in some place like Tanzania and dig up dead bodies."

Gertie looked at her awkwardly. "That's interesting."

"Seriously," Mary went on, "when I grow up, I want to be a paleoanthropologist, that's someone who studies the skeletons of early humans—dead of course!"

"Oh," Gertie said, understanding. "Sounds like a good job."

"Thank you," Mary said, touching Gertie's cloak. "I can't believe how authentic your costume looks, like it really came from ancient Africa!"

"Well," Gertie grinned, thinking it best not to admit that it actually was from ancient Africa, "I hope you get to dig up every-*body* you want someday."

Mary laughed. "Everyone tells me the desert is no place for girls."

Gertie remembered bouncing along on the elephant that had rescued her from the battle. "A girl has to rely on her instincts, Mary."

"Do you trust yours, Gertie?"

"It's how I've stayed alive this long."

Mary was impressed. "Are you some kind of explorer then?"

"I suppose so. . . ."

"And what do you want to do when *you* grow up, Gertie?"

An entire field's worth of vegetables had been arranged on the buffet table in the shape of a face, with radishes for lips, celery for a nose, and black olive eyes. To avoid answering, Gertie grabbed a cauliflower ear and began chewing.

In a way, Gertie felt she trusted Mary enough to tell her *everything*. Just blurt it out. Perhaps Mary might even know something, or be able to help in some way? She felt uneasy about having to lie to her new friend. She couldn't say anything about Skuldark, the Time Cat—or even Robot Rabbit Boy. Which was a shame, since she thought Mary would have liked the little creature.

"Oh, well, I'm not sure yet," Gertie said, trying to sound sincere. "Tell me more about Tanzania. . . ."

But Mary was busy waving to someone on the other side of the room. A tall woman in a ball gown with gloves that went up to her elbow.

"Sorry, but Mummy is here," Mary said, putting down her plate. "I'm afraid I have to leave."

"Oh no!"

Mary extended a gloved hand. "You're a true flapper in my opinion. It was so nice to meet you, Gertrude—oh," she said, noticing Gertie's watch, "where did you get that?"

"The watch?"

"Yes! My mother's friend Mercedes has one just like it!" Mary continued. "But she lost it."

Gertie's eyes opened very wide.

"Mercedes Gleitze?" she asked casually. "The champion swimmer?"

"Yes! She had a lucky watch just like that, but lost it a few days ago. She was very upset. There's a party upstairs for her as she's going to swim the English Channel tomorrow."

"Oh, I'd love to meet her!" Gertie said, thinking quickly. "Will you introduce me?"

"I'm afraid that's impossible," Mary said. "Immediately after her speech, she left for Croydon Airport, where Imperial Airways had a de Havilland 34 waiting to fly her to Cap Gris Nez in France for tomorrow's swim."

"But it's urgent!" Gertie cried. "I have to get her . . . autograph!"

"Then you'll need wings!" Mary laughed. "Farewell, Gertrude Milk."

Even though Gertie had only known Mary for a short time, she felt the weight of their parting. They would probably never meet again.

"Take these!" Gertie said, fumbling for the tickets she had been given earlier by the friendly American clown. "Maybe you can take your mother to a show?"

"How utterly decent of you," Mary said. "How sporting! I've read all about Mr. Fred Astaire in *The Tatler*; it's supposed to be a hoot."

Gertie blushed as her new friend gave her a kiss and held her hand.

"I must say I'm going to miss you," Mary said. "And I never say that to *anyone*." She removed a peacock feather that was attached to her costume.

"A gift . . ." she said, passing it to Gertie. "Flappers forever?"

Gertie twirled the feather in her hand as Mary disappeared into the crowd toward her mother.

"Flappers forever," Gertie whispered, realizing that loss was a feeling she would have to get used to, if she accepted her fate as a Keeper.

When Mary reached her mother, Gertie watched them embrace. She could only imagine what nice motherly things were being said. They would go to the show and see Mr. Astaire dance. Sit close to each other and laugh. Then walk home holding hands, or stop somewhere for hot chocolate and watch the trams. Gertie turned the peacock feather in her hands, trying to imagine the sensation of having a mother and a home.

But underneath this desire for comfort, Gertie felt something else, something exciting, dangerous, and irresistible, just bubbling beneath the surface. It was not only a determination to help Kolt and do the right thing—but the need for action, a life of thrilling adventures and new things.

Gertie realized then that such feelings were *also* a part of who she was. She would never stop looking for her family, she knew that—but in the meantime, why not live the way she felt was right? And if that meant returning things to the world, then that's exactly what she was going to do.

Gertie stormed out of the ballroom and found a staircase that led upstairs. When a waiter tried to block her path to the Palm Court, she simply kept walking and barked, "Out of my way!"

He moved swiftly to one side.

25

The Passage Behind the Painting

GERTIE FOUND KOLT dozing on a blue velvet sofa in the hotel lobby. She tapped his shoulder with gentle urgency.

"Where am I?" he mumbled. "What's going on?"

"We're in London at the Ritz Hotel, why are you sleeping? We're on a mission."

Kolt opened his eyes and soon recovered a sense of urgency. "Yes, yes, you're right, we're here to return the watch, not to dance and gobble charcoal crackers with delicious smears of vegetarian pâté."

Gertie explained how their champion swimmer was on her way to the coast of France, where she planned to swim across the sea at dawn. "So I think we've missed our chance," she said, "unless we come up with a plan."

"Why on earth would she want to swim across the sea?"

"Because," Gertie pointed out, "she's a brave, independent, and free-spirited woman: a flapper."

"Oh, a flapper! In that case," Kolt said, "swimming the English Channel makes perfect sense. Do you still have the watch?"

Gertie held up her wrist. "Of course I do. Aren't you listening to me?"

Kolt studied the timepiece. "If only there were some clue to how a return might be possible under the current time constraints."

"I wonder why it's so important?" Gertie said, noticing the word OYSTER written on the dial. "I suppose if it helps Mercedes Gleitze complete the swim, that might inspire women all over the world to follow *their* dreams!"

Kolt agreed. "Many of the things the B.D.B.U. has me return to the world appear quite ordinary. But you never know if the dirty feather might turn out to be Shakespeare's favorite quill, or a dried-up tube of paint is for Frida Kahlo's next masterpiece. The B.D.B.U. has its reasons."

Gertie suggested racing to the coast in the Time Cat and then finding some kind of small but fast boat to get them to France.

"If only the Time Cat were also a Time Tuna," Gertie said, trying to think of anything that would get them to France on time.

But Kolt admitted they had hardly any fuel in the car and no emergency rockets. It was also the middle of the night, they were both tired, and the model Jaguar they were driving would not be invented for another forty years or so.

"Parking it on a side street is one thing, Gertie, but driving it through England for several hours is another matter, even if we had enough fuel."

"We can't go back to Skuldark. We have to find a way!"

"But we only have seven hours left, and not a penny of local money."

Gertie was adamant. "I want to do what we came here to do, which is give this woman what belongs to her. It's my first solo mission, and I'm not giving up."

Kolt smiled. "Well it sounds like you've become a bit of a flapper yourself."

Gertie collapsed onto the blue sofa next to Kolt. "C'mon! Let's think of something. . . ."

A teenage waiter appeared with Earl Grey tea for two and several bars of the Ritz Hotel's crumbly biscotti.

"Complimentary after-party refreshments, sir and miss," he said.

"We'll walk to the south coast then!" Gertie said jumping up. "We'll go on foot, and then get on a fishing boat to France."

The waiter smirked. "Walk to Dover, miss? That's over seventy miles away!"

Gertie slumped down between two fat cushions. "That far?"

"At least that far," said the waiter. "But a very nice walk if you have a few days . . . just follow the Thames River west, until Gravesend, then continue in a straight line southwest toward the famous Chatham Dockyard, then follow the coast to Whitstable, then turn right, and go through Canterbury—visit the cathedral if you have time—then on to the white cliffs of Dover. If you had a longer period in which to holiday, you could follow the coast all the way around; it would be lovely if only for the birds you'd see."

"Wow!" Gertie said. "You're like a human map!"

The waiter blushed. "Well, thank you, miss, I inherited my father's passion for adventure."

"Would you write all that down for me?" Gertie asked him kindly. "And if you know any places we could get on a boat to France, that would be really helpful too."

"You mean, draw you a map?" the waiter asked eagerly.

Gertie nodded politely. "If you don't mind."

The waiter took a hotel pencil from his pocket, and sketched the route carefully on the back of a cloth napkin. His drawing included the names of towns, villages, and landmarks. He even wrote "Good Luck!" at the bottom, along with his name, Edward Shackleton.

Gertie thanked the clever waiter as he walked away.

"It's no use," Kolt said. "We'd have to walk at fifteen miles per hour at least, then find a water craft immediately. It's impossible, I'm afraid."

Gertie stared at the napkin in her hand. The reality of

their situation was beginning to sink in. "Seems a shame to waste such a beautiful map."

"I'd expect nothing less from one of the Shackleton family."

"The waiter?"

"Oh, yes, in about forty-five years, he'll be president of the Royal Geographical Society. His father was Ernest Shackleton, an explorer who I'm sorry to say perished on his way to the South Pole not long ago."

Gertie folded the map into her cloak. "But there *must* be a way!" she insisted, gritting her teeth. "If I fail, I'm helping the Losers destroy human life by unleashing chaos and ignorance."

"Don't be too hard on yourself, Gertie, it's only one mission. Remember our motto, it could—"

"I know. . . ." She sighed, rubbing the head of the golden goat lamp next to her. "I know."

Then to her astonishment, the goat's eyes blinked three times, and behind the couch a tall painting swung open to reveal a passageway.

Kolt was amazed. "I find as a Keeper of Lost Things that when secret doorways or portals open up, it's generally a good idea to go through them."

"Come on then," Gertie said. "What are we waiting for?"

Kolt grabbed a handful of biscotti and they disappeared through a hole in the wall.

26

The Mayfly Catapult

At the top of a dark, narrow staircase, Gertie and Kolt were met by a uniformed attendant wearing a top hat and white gloves. He saluted immediately.

"On behalf of His Majesty, George the Fifth," he said, "what is your wish?"

"Our wish?" Kolt said, rubbing his chin. "Oh dear, I haven't wished for anything in ages."

This seemed to make the guard nervous. "I didn't mean *wish* in the way one reads about them in fairy tales, sir, but rather as a polite way of letting you know that I'm here to help."

Kolt nudged Gertie. "See what I told you about the British? Impeccable manners."

"Our wish," Gertie said boldly, "is to get to Cap Gris Nez as quickly as we can."

"Yes, ma'am," said the guard, clicking the heels of his

patent leather Oxford shoes. "The French coast as soon as possible. Please follow me at once."

Gertie couldn't believe it worked. *Perhaps I am a flapper after all*, she thought.

The guard led them through a door and into a cupboard of brooms, dustpans, and tickling feather dusters (which made everyone laugh for a minute), then through a low door that led to another staircase.

"May I ask where you're taking us?" Kolt said, as there was now a terrible whirring noise that seemed to be getting louder with each ascending step.

"To the roof!" he said. "As secret agents in the service of His Majesty, you both have unrestricted access to the Mayfly—a perk of the job."

"A Mayfly!" Kolt joked. "Well, I hope it doesn't bite!"

"Well, sir, it would only bite if you didn't know how to operate it," the guard chuckled. "In that case, it would mean you were enemy spies, and I would have to dispose of you both immediately once we got to the roof."

Gertie and Kolt laughed nervously.

The buzzing was now so loud that when they finally got to the top of the Ritz Hotel it was impossible to say anything without screaming.

To Gertie's amazement, the Mayfly turned out to be a bright yellow two-seater biplane, with its propeller already spinning furiously.

"Get in!" shouted the guard, moving toward a mechanism with several levers. On the wall Gertie spotted a sign.

MODERATE DANGER OF DEATH
CATAPULT RELEASE MECHANISM

"C'mon!" she said, pulling Kolt toward the cockpit.

"What are you doing?" he mouthed over the roar of the aircraft engine.

"We have to try! It's the only way to complete my first mission!"

"G-G-Gertie!" he stammered. "We don't know how to fly *any* aircraft—let alone one held together by chopsticks!"

"Trust me!"

The guard was now starting to get suspicious, so Kolt had no choice but to follow Gertie and buckle into the backseat of the Mayfly, strapping on some goggles he found lying on the seat.

Gertie placed her hands on the controls and, with an enormous grin, nodded to the guard to release the catapult. The force at which they were flung into the midnight sky was so great that both Keepers were unable to breathe for several seconds as their stomachs crunched with the sudden velocity.

By the time Gertie realized what had happened, the Ritz Hotel was just a dark lump with bright little squares far below. The Mayfly motor vibrated like ten thousand wasps trapped in a metal box. When Gertie pulled on the level, the nose of the aircraft lurched upward, and when she moved it left, the plane banked steeply.

"I think I'm getting the hang of it!" she announced,

hardly able to believe what was happening. But when she turned around, Kolt's mouth was fixed open in a silent scream.

She adjusted the flaps, took note of the wind direction, made a compass reading, and carefully looked at the map the waiter had drawn, holding on tight so it didn't blow away.

To both her own and Kolt's utter disbelief, Gertie was flying a 1920s biplane. Her hands just knew how to move on the controls, how to steer and maintain altitude. She even knew how to read the night sky for direction.

Then Gertie remembered something.

"Sopwith Camel!" she bellowed. "Sopwith Camel!"

"What?" shouted Kolt. "Are we getting low on oxygen? I feel quite faint."

"No," shouted Gertie, "back in the desert when I remembered the word 'camel' from my old life?"

Kolt nodded.

"Well, it wasn't the animal! It was an aircraft! A Sopwith Camel!"

"That's right . . . a Sopwith Camel *is* an airplane."

"Yes!" Gertie cried, "I must be some kind of child pilot, because I'm flying! My hands and arms remember how to do it, even if I can't remember my own name. I must have been the pilot of a Sopwith Camel!"

With London now just a distant nest of flickering gaslights miles behind them, Gertie followed the Thames River by the reflection of moonlight on the water.

Cold dark air rushed through the cockpit. Gertie had to keep moving her arms and legs so she could feel them. But neither Keeper could stop peering up at the glittering night sky, sprayed generously with stars.

Their bodies soared in the open-top Mayfly as they cleared the white cliffs of Dover and roared out over the deep sea. The sense of freedom was exhilarating.

The Mayfly was faster than Gertie thought, and soon they were circling over a dark mass that Kolt said was probably France. When they descended to get a closer look, Gertie noticed a crowd of people standing under gray cliffs in the murky light.

She motioned to Kolt. "Must be Cap Gris Nez!"

From the air it was easy to spot the place where the champion swimmer Mercedes Gleitze intended to enter the water. Flags had been put up, and a group of well-wishers and newspaper photographers had clustered together with their equipment.

Gertie pulled up and steered inland, looking for a strip of solid ground where they could touch down on the Mayfly's thin, dinner-plate wheels.

"Brace yourself!" she called out as they began a steep descent over some low trees.

Gertie's hands moved quickly over all the levers and switches as they landed with a heavy thud in a cow field.

Gertie and Kolt climbed out of the aircraft quickly and began jumping about to get the blood flowing in their freezing bodies. The cows had moved to one side of the field and stared with fear and fascination, their hot breath steaming in the cold dawn air.

"That was amazing!" Kolt said. "You really are a pilot!"

For a few moments, Gertie was so cold it was hard to talk. She vowed never to fly again without warm clothes. Kolt was also suffering but found that dancing around in circles was the most effective cure for frozen limbs.

Once blood was flowing, they hurried over the cold pasture, past the cows, toward the sea.

"I'm just imagining," Kolt said. "A roaring hot fire with warm winter moonberry juice and buttered toast."

"And peach cake!"

They were soon trudging across smooth, shiny pebbles and moving toward a crowd of people who were staring out into thick fog, which lingered in the predawn darkness. In the distance, a fishing vessel's fog horn wailed. Despite her feet feeling like cold bricks, Gertie rushed into the group.

"Where's Mercedes?" she asked a long-faced woman holding a notepad. The woman pointed with her fountain pen.

"Somewhere out there, dear, in the watery darkness."

"What? She's gone?"

"About five minutes ago."

"But I have to see her!"

"Then you'll have to swim the channel too." She laughed.

Gertie pulled off her North African cloth shoes and tumbled down the stones to the water.

"I was only joking!" called the woman. "Girl! Girl!"

Kolt was calling after her too, and there were gasps from

the onlookers. The frigid water on her bare legs was nothing compared to the sting of her failure. But when Gertie got up to her knees, she found that she could not continue. The water was too icy, and the cold rocks were so slippery under her feet she could barely stand. Kolt waded in and plucked her from the waves that crashed and sprayed them both with freezing water.

When they were back on the rocky beach, Gertie lay on the damp stones and stared out into the darkness, too angry to cry. She couldn't believe that she had endured all that for nothing.

The group of journalists and well-wishers soon dispersed, and Gertie was alone with Kolt.

"If only Johnny the Guard Worm were here," Kolt sighed. "We might have had a chance of catching up."

"I failed," Gertie said weakly.

Kolt patted her on the back. "It happens. Returning things to the world is not a perfect science. Life gets in the way."

But then the tone of his voice shifted and was suddenly not so forgiving.

"I'm afraid there's no nice way to tell you this," he went on, "but in addition to failing to return an object, you've also broken one of the Keepers' most important rules."

Gertie couldn't believe what she was hearing.

"What rule?"

"We've been here ten hours and forty-nine minutes. In approximately eleven minutes, we're both going to get snatched."

"So let's use the time machine!" Gertie cried.

"Be my guest," Kolt said. "It's your mission."

Gertie fumbled in her pockets and realized she had forgotten to bring the time machine and key. More bitter disappointment. The first and most important rule of being a Keeper, and she'd broken it.

"What will happen now?" she asked in a small, sad voice.

"Well, the Time Cat will eventually find its way back to Skuldark, as it is now technically lost. Hopefully the key and time machine will still be in the glove box where we left them, but if there were any Losers hanging around, it could mean major trouble."

"I really failed," Gertie said, picking up a few of the beach stones. She let them drop, one by one. "I messed everything up on my first go."

"Are you fully aware of how serious the situation is with the time machine and key?"

Gertie nodded. She could feel tears gathering but was determined not to cry. *At least I can fly a plane,* she thought, but knew she was just saying it to make herself feel better.

"Do you feel like on future missions, Gertie, you will have an understanding of how important it is to be mindful of time limits?"

"Yes, I could never forget," Gertie said miserably. "But it doesn't help us now. I still have the watch, and we're about to get snatched."

"Do you feel you've learned the importance of never, ever, ever traveling too far from the Time Cat, or more importantly, from the time machine and key?"

"Definitely," Gertie said. "All I wanted was to leave Skuldark, but now I would do anything to get back there." She looked up at Kolt. "Without getting snatched, I mean."

Kolt seemed satisfied. "Well, it seems you've learned your lesson."

Then out of his pocket came the time machine and Keepers' key.

Gertie almost fainted with relief. "You brought them!"

"While I was waiting for you to find me in the hotel, I ran back to the Time Cat and grabbed them, just in case," Kolt beamed. "It is *my* key, after all, so it's not completely your fault—"

"But if only I'd left the party sooner. If only . . ."

"Not every mission will be successful, Gertie. Failing is a part of life, even for Keepers. The important thing is to keep going."

Gertie knew he was right, but was too mad at herself to admit it.

"By the way," Kolt said, "if that metal creature is still stuck to the bumper of the Time Cat, we'll have to decide what to do with it."

"It's not a metal creature," argued Gertie, getting some of her energy back, "it's a Robot Rabbit Boy Series 7. . . ."

Kolt turned his key in the small wooden box, and they linked arms to be zapped over the graviton bridge. "And I think," Gertie continued saying, "he's cuuuuuuuttttttttttte. . . ."

27

A Terrifying Discovery

DURING A LONG BUBBLE BATH back at the cottage, Gertie sank down in the deep, warm water, so her eyes were at the same level as the suds.

She thought about all the things that had happened—not only since arriving on Skuldark, but on their adventure to ancient Alexandria when she collapsed in the desert, then breaking down on planet Earth after humans had left, where the trees were seven miles high and there were robot animal children roaming about with no one to play with. She had also made a friend, and understood how the objects she returned were symbols of hope and human achievement.

Gertie remembered returning to the cottage to fetch supplies to repair the Time Cat. How it felt to be alone again. And the feeling of being trusted with an important task.

She had learned that she was some kind of pilot and had great skill with open-top aircraft of the early twentieth century—not only the Halton Mayfly they borrowed from the king of England, but another type of airplane called a Sopwith Camel. Gertie decided she would hunt for a picture of the airplane in one of Kolt's books.

Although she still felt ashamed at having failed her first mission, she couldn't stop remembering the rush of excitement while exploring the abandoned city of Los Angeles. It felt like an arrow pointing toward the truth of who she was.

Gertie imagined her family living on Earth, in Los Angeles before the evacuation. She pictured herself running through the streets. The dinosaur apple trees would not have been planted yet, and the city would have been filled with heat and light and brightly colored cars.

After her bath, Gertie changed into a pair of green pajamas from the Sock Drawer and got into bed. Kolt said the Time Cat would arrive sometime in the night. Before closing her eyes Gertie looked around her darkened room, imagining all the different places her new friend (if he was still frozen to the bumper) might like to sleep, and if his eyes would glow, and how pleased he would be to have his paws and ears washed with a soft cloth and some warm, soapy water.

After a long night of deep sleep, Gertie dressed and rushed out to the kitchen. Kolt was wearing red corduroy trousers, a black T-shirt, and navy blazer with brass buttons. He was sitting before a plate of warm scones, a pot of tea, several open jars of jam, and a silver hair dryer.

Gertie could barely control her excitement. "Did the Time Cat come back? Is the—"

Kolt motioned with his eyes to a folded blanket on the floor, where a Series 7 robot animal child was snoring away, with several kinds of sticky jam on his paws.

"He was still a bit frozen when the Time Cat appeared around sunrise, so I used this silly thing from 1984," he said, pointing to the silver hair dryer on the table. "Then I let him dip his paw into whichever jam looked good—which turned out to be all of them."

"Is he fully . . . defrosted?"

"I think so."

"What happened when he came around?"

"I fed him, then tickled his belly, and he went right to sleep."

"So he likes jam. . . ." Gertie mused, looking at the open jars.

"The B.D.B.U. doesn't allow for passengers, Gertie, but as he hasn't disappeared yet, robot rabbit children might turn out to be an exception."

"I'd better study that book I found on the Series 7," Gertie said. "Though how hard can it be to look after a little cute robot rabbit boy? I can probably just skim the pages. We already know he likes fruit jam."

"I glanced over the manual this morning," Kolt said.

"Apparently they pick up words that sound useful and try to communicate using those."

Gertie inspected the sleeping figure and watched its metal belly move up and down with each rabbity snore.

"So does it know any words?"

"It kept saying 'eggcup', and 'lavender,' and offering me 'dollops of mashed potatoes.' That must be all it knows."

"Well, I'll teach it more," Gertie said. "Oh, I hope the B.D.B.U. doesn't send him back!"

"Mrs. Pumble brought a lost kitten here once, just a tiny scrap of fur it was! Well, that cat lived for almost a century in a wicker basket beside the fire. Doris was her name."

"Well, if Doris was allowed to stay, perhaps I should ask the B.D.B.U. if we can keep Robot Rabbit Boy!"

"Go up there after breakfast and tell the book your wish. Perhaps it'll turn to a page that offers some advice!" Kolt said. "It's worth a try, and the B.D.B.U. adores you."

"I wish I could ask it who I am," Gertie said.

Kolt laughed good-naturedly. "I must have tried that a thousand times."

Just then, there was a tremendous bang from the garden. Gertie jumped in shock and rushed over to the window.

"What was that?"

Kolt didn't seem worried. "It's probably just the tangle of bicycles shifting again, or part of the cliff giving way. It happens from time to time. I'll go out there a bit later and check."

"But it was so loud!"

"Things collapsing in the garden have become a normal part of Keeper life in the Age of Disappearance, Gertie. In fact, we should probably wear helmets out there from now on . . . at least until we're clear of the garden."

Gertie returned to the table and sat down.

"Am I allowed to go past the garden? Is the island safe to explore?"

"Mostly," Kolt said, "in the daylight—and there's really a lot to see, such as the ruined village of Keepers past, and Ravens' Peak."

"But it's dangerous at night, right? Because of the giant millipedes."

"There are some risks," Kolt said, "but not from millipedes; I just made those up so you wouldn't run off."

"You mean there are no teeth-grinding millipedes waiting to devour me? Then what were those glowing things I saw?"

Kolt grinned. "Wild moonberries!"

"And what about creatures that rip apart the letters of their own names, so no one knows they exist—are they real?"

"How would I know?" Kolt said. "But the island does have its inhabitants: Attacoppes, for instance, sea monsters of varying sizes, the Fern Valley Banshee, and those big, lumbering creatures that live down on the plains near the ruined village. There are also the tunnels of Bodwin, which Mrs. Pumble always told me to stay away from, so what lives in those is a mystery even to me."

When the scones had been reduced to moist crumbs,

and the teapot contained nothing but wet tea leaves, Gertie stroked the soft ragged ear of sleeping Robot Rabbit Boy and then went over to the mantelpiece and slid out *The History of Chickens.*

After slipping through the secret entrance, she climbed the steps to the B.D.B.U., where she would beg the old book to let Robot Rabbit Boy stay.

It didn't seem as far to the top as the first time, and, when she arrived at the door, Gertie lay her hand flat against the wood and stood back as the heavy wood slowly rose.

Then she spoke the phrase, "It could always be worse!" and the second metal door began to separate. But before it was completely open, Gertie sensed that something was wrong.

First, she smelled burning—as though someone had lit paper on fire. Then she noticed the room was dark, when sunlight should have been streaming in through the many windows.

After entering cautiously, Gertie stood frozen with horror. The wooden steps leading up to the B.D.B.U. had been smashed to bits, as though stomped by an enormous foot. Her eyes darted to the stone pedestal that was black and cratered, as though an explosion had taken place on top of it. Where the B.D.B.U. had once majestically rested, its pages bright and glowing, there was now only scorched stone, with a cloud of lingering smoke.

The B.D.B.U. was gone. Not just gone, but stolen.

28

Intruders

KOLT WAS IN HIS WORKSHOP, cutting wood to make small ladders for Robot Rabbit Boy, when Gertie burst in. She was so out of breath it was hard to speak.

"It's gone!" she gasped. "It's ... not ... there!"

Kolt dropped the tool that was in his hand. "Gone? Robot Ra—"

"The ... B.D.B.U. ... . it's ... not ... there," Gertie cried out. "The B.D.B.U. is missing! Blown up! Burned out! Stolen!"

Kolt's face turned completely white.

"No!" he stammered. "It can't be!"

When they reached the top of the tower, Kolt rushed in and inspected the stone pedestal that was still charred and smoking.

"Oh this is bad!" He shook his head gravely. "This is very, very bad."

"Has it ever happened before? Maybe it's lost?"

"It's definitely been stolen," he said, closing his eyes. "The source of all knowledge in the universe has been swiped from right under our noses. This is the work of the Losers."

"But the door was closed when I came up here! I had to use my hand print to gain entrance."

"I don't understand," Kolt said. "But it doesn't matter, we're going to have to give chase. The pursued must become the pursuer! Action is eloquence!"

They rushed back downstairs, where Robot Rabbit Boy had woken up and was binky-jumping with excitement to see Gertie.

"Eggcup! Eggcup! Eggcup!"

Gertie scooped him into her arms. "I'm glad you're awake, but there's an emergency going on because a group of very bad people have stolen something precious."

"A dollop of mashed potato?"

"No, something much more important than a crushed vegetable."

Kolt paced up and down, muttering to himself, trying to devise a plan to rescue the old book.

"Maybe we try to find out where they've been hiding?" Gertie suggested.

"We have no way of knowing where that might be. They

could be headquartered at any point in history, depending on Vispoth's calculations."

Gertie thought for a minute.

"If I were the B.D.B.U.," she said slowly, "and I needed rescuing, I would summon the Keepers by demanding the return of something from where I was being kept prisoner!"

"—Thus reuniting Keepers and book!" Kolt rattled off excitedly. "That's brilliant, Gertie! Let's go under the house and see if the cave sprites have noticed anything glowing, vibrating, or bouncing around. That could be it!"

He swept the rug from over the trapdoor, then jumped back in horror.

"Noooo!" he roared. "No, no, no, no! We're doomed."

Gertie scrambled over with Robot Rabbit Boy still in her arms like a fluffy baby.

Kolt was hysterical. "They've gotten under the cottage! And locked the trapdoor behind them!"

Gertie bent down and examined an enormous combination padlock of shiny black metal, with thousands of digital numbers scrolling over its surface.

"What kind of lock is this?" she asked.

"A Flux Bandit," Kolt groaned. "A Japanese padlock from the middle of the twenty-third century that's impossible to break. Those numbers you see flashing over the metal are all variants of the combination, which changes one hundred times a second. If only we could get it off—then at least we'd know if they stole anything from downstairs, and perhaps get hold of an item that will lead us to where the B.D.B.U. has been taken."

Gertie glared at the numbers flashing silently over the black steel. "There must be a way!"

"It's no use," Kolt said. "Everybody knows the Flux Bandit is indestructible."

Gertie was holding Robot Rabbit Boy in one arm when he began to wriggle. She put him down, and he hopped over to the trapdoor casually, his metal legs clinking.

"Eggcup?" he said, touching the padlock with his paw.

"Poor little creature," Kolt said. "He probably thinks it's a toy."

Robot Rabbit Boy sniffed the lock, then looked up at Kolt with his nose twitching. "A dollop of mashed potato?"

Kolt smiled. "I would love a dollop of mashed potato—but first we have to think of a way to get past the most secure, sophisticated, unbreakable superpadlock ever made, which I'm afraid is impossible. There's nothing in the entire universe that can penetrate such an impenetrable mechanism."

Robot Rabbit Boy touched the Flux Bandit again, his nose still twitching like mad.

"That's strange," Kolt said. "I wonder what he's doing."

Gertie couldn't figure it out either. "Maybe he's about to sneeze?"

Then suddenly, from out of nowhere, a bolt of high-intensity, scorching-hot laser-beam shot from the little x mark below Robot Rabbit Boy's nose, and in a flash of blinding light the kitchen was sprayed by thousands of exploding Flux Bandit pieces.

Robot Rabbit Boy pointed at the blackened, smoldering hole in the floor with his paw. "A dollop of eggcup."

"B-b-b-big . . . d-d-dollop." Kolt whimpered, his hair blown back from the explosion.

Gertie patted her little friend on the head, then turned to Kolt through the smoky air.

"Guess I'd better read the instruction manual after all."

29

A Big Moment for Robot Rabbit Boy

As they raced down the basement stairs, Gertie saw something ahead of her glowing.

"Stop! Stop!" she called back to the others. "There's something on the step." But then she recognized what it was.

"Slug Lamp!"

"What on earth is that doing down here?" Kolt said, catching up. "Moonberries don't grow underground."

Gertie picked it up and looked at its squashy, sluggy face.

"Hey! It's the one you gave me on my first night here!"

At hearing her voice, the Slug Lamp glowed a bit brighter.

"Throw it upstairs through the trapdoor," Kolt said quickly. "We have work to do."

"I will not!" Gertie snapped. "I'll bet it was trying to save the cave sprites, but only got as far as the third step."

The Slug Lamp glowed and wriggled as if this were all true. Robot Rabbit Boy stepped down to where Gertie was and touched the creature with his paw.

"Mashed potato?"

"Slug Lamp," Gertie said, then stuffed the creature into her jeans pocket where he'd be safe. "C'mon, let's go!"

Once they were in the basement, the presence of intruders was immediately clear. Most of the lamps had been pulled from the rock and lay glowing in bits on the ground. Messages had also been spray painted on the cave walls, such as:

loserz win!

And:

wee no wear u live!

And perhaps the one they had intended to be most frightening but wasn't:

keepers dye

A few of the bedroom doors had cracks and indentations where they had been thumped with something hard and heavy.

"Look, Kolt! They must have tried to get into some of the rooms."

"But they couldn't, could they?" Kolt said, examining the handles. "I wonder why their stolen Keepers' key didn't work?"

"I guess the same reason they couldn't get into our bedrooms.... Maybe the B.D.B.U. has the power to block them!"

"Yes, or maybe they only work when yielded by a true Keeper."

The Losers had also failed to capture, or douse, even a single cave sprite, and the whole *week* of them appeared to meet Gertie and Kolt as a chaotic jumble of orange lights, although old Sunday still lagged behind, confused as to what was happening.

Robot Rabbit Boy couldn't stop looking at the sprites. "Eggcup ..." he said dreamily, reaching up with his ragged paw toward the lowest one. "Lavender ..."

"Thank goodness they're unharmed!" Kolt said, wondering why the sprites had begun to hover over an ancient Inuit boat in the center of the room. "What are they doing?"

"Maybe they have something to show us?" Gertie asked.

"That's it, you're right!" Kolt said, rushing over to the boat. "Let's get in the umiak! The sprites must want to take us deep under the cliff to one of the lowest rooms. Climb inside the boat, everyone!"

Gertie and Robot Rabbit Boy stepped sheepishly inside the vessel—which Kolt said had been joined from whalebone and animal skins by the native people of Greenland.

"Hold on, both of you," he instructed.

"Mashed potato?"

"But there's no water up here," Gertie pointed out, looking around, "so hooooowwww—"

A trapdoor opened suddenly under the umiak, dropping the boat and its crew of three ten feet into a fast-flowing underground river.

"Hold on for dear life!" Kolt bellowed over the thunder of rushing water. "If anything jumps into the boat—throw it out!"

They were going so fast, Gertie didn't even try to answer. She just gripped the sides, her hair blowing wildly as they dropped through a series of corkscrew turns. All Gertie could do was blink away the splashing water as best she could and hope that Robot Rabbit Boy hadn't bounced out of the boat. When a sharp corner threw them all to the side of the bone-framed kayak, Gertie felt the Slug Lamp squirming in her pocket. Then a wave of freezing water took her breath away.

Finally, they dropped from the rushing tunnel into a deep lagoon.

Everyone was sopping wet, but had somehow managed to stay in the boat during the hellish descent. As they drifted with the current, still recovering their senses, Gertie saw they were deep under the cliff, most likely at sea level.

"We made it!" she said, taking the Slug Lamp out of her pocket to check if it was okay. The squashy creature nodded and blinked its eyes.

Kolt grabbed a bone oar and rowed them to the side of the cave. With the cave sprites drifting overhead, there was enough light for Gertie to make out a rocky staircase leading to a corridor lined with doors.

"That must be it!"

They clambered out of the boat and ran up the steps.

"It's bedroom 888," said Kolt, jostling his key into the lock. With extreme caution Kolt, Gertie, Robot Rabbit Boy, the Slug Lamp (in Gertie's pocket), and cave sprites entered the darkened chamber.

To Gertie's great relief, it didn't appear to be a *living* room (like the bedroom of lost limbs), as all they could see at first were narrow slits of bamboo with vertical writing that had been tied together with string.

"Books," Kolt said, unrolling one. "Old Chinese books."

"Why are there books in here?"

"I don't know," Kolt said. "But not all books contain knowledge, Gertie—some are just pamphlets intended to spread fear."

Gertie pointed to a plain-looking bowl with pink powder. "I thought each room contained only one type of thing?"

"This one is different," Kolt said apprehensively. "I knew it existed, but hoped I'd never see it."

"Why?"

"Because bedroom 888 contains an object from ancient Asia capable of destroying the B.D.B.U."

"It can be destroyed?"

"Oh yes . . . just like any living thing."

"But why these things?"

"Because they're made from metals, or powders, or even sound frequencies that have been known to undo the fibers from which the B.D.B.U. is woven. The rooms in this lower chamber of the cliff contain some of the most dangerous items from the world."

Gertie stared in awe at the various artifacts capable of such devastation. There was a bronze gong with a skull drawn on it, three green poles sharpened at the edges, a statue of an angry looking half-man/half-fish, a glass ball with fire inside, and a sword in a sheath woven with silver, which was the only item in the room glowing brightly.

Kolt saw it too.

"Be careful!" he said. "Stay back, and let the cave sprites do their job."

"Why would the B.D.B.U. want us to get something that could destroy it?" Gertie asked. "It doesn't make sense."

They watched as the cave sprites flitted about the room over the many objects, before finally settling on the glowing sword.

"Could it be wrong?" Gertie asked. "You said the B.D.B.U. sometimes gets things mixed up, so how can we be sure?"

When the cave sprites had gone over the ancient weapon several times, checking to make sure it wasn't a trap left by the Losers, Kolt stepped forward and took hold of it. "At this point we have no choice, Gertie. It's blind faith in the old book from here on out."

Gertie and Robot Rabbit Boy followed Kolt out of

bedroom 888, and watched as he removed his key from the lock, then hurriedly took out the time machine.

"We're not going in the Time Cat?"

"No time!" Kolt said. "We'd have to paddle out of the cliff, then around to the beach. Even with Johnny the Guard Worm pushing us, it would take too long to get back to the garden."

"Do you know where we're going?"

"Ancient China, I think, but I don't know exactly, sometime between 700 and 300 B.C.E. We're going to have to trust that the B.D.B.U. knows what it's doing."

"Shouldn't we change clothes at least, to fit in?" Gertie said.

"We can't visit the Sock Drawer, we've got Losers to catch! Now everybody link hands."

With the Slug Lamp still in her pocket, Gertie huddled next to Kolt as he threaded his key into the time machine.

"Wait!" she cried, looking around for Robot Rabbit Boy, who had slinked off to a far corner of the cave.

"What's he doing?" Kolt called out. "Robot Rabbit Boy! Over here now! Eggcup! Eggcup!"

But he just stood there, looking down at the floor and shuffling his paws.

"He's upset about something," Gertie said. "Maybe he thinks we're taking him back to the abandoned city?"

"I'll take care of this," Kolt said, giving Gertie the sword and rushing over to the little creature.

"Down on one knee!"

Robot Rabbit Boy did as he was told, his plump metal legs knocking with fear.

"I, Kolt, head Keeper of Skuldark, hereby officially recognize that the Series 7 creature known as Robot Rabbit Boy is to be sworn in by an emergency honorary decree in the Age of Disappearance as an official Keeper of Lost Things, thus enjoying all the privileges, benefits, protections, mysteries, coincidences, extraordinary cakes, and dangers accompanying the aforementioned position, from now until the end—or the beginning—of time. Upon these words I do so solemnly swear, this day, with Gertie Milk as my official witness . . . *now link up!*"

30

Evil in the Forest of Moganshan

WITH A FLASH OF BLUE LIGHT, they cleared the graviton bridge and found themselves in a dense green forest of bamboo and pine. The cool air was alive with birdsong and the rattle of cicadas from low branches. Wind swayed the hollow bamboo trunks, making them knock.

"It's Asia for sure," Kolt said, "but when, I can't say."

"I wish you had let me change clothes!" complained Gertie. "I don't think there was denim in ancient Asia, and I'm still wet from that weird bone canoe."

Kolt shot her a look of annoyance. "You might be more concerned about the fact that we have a robot rabbit who can shoot high-powered laser beams from the little x below his nose. That might draw a *bit* more attention than your wet jeans."

"Right," Gertie said, looking down into her little friend's eyes, which glowed neon purple.

"Now let's *really* concentrate on what to do, because if we don't get the B.D.B.U. back, human achievements will soon disappear most likely along with us, and our species will be doomed to—"

"The age of ignorance!" Gertie interrupted.

"I'm afraid so," Kolt said, "with people burning witches again."

"There are witches?"

"Thank goodness yes. . . . Mrs. Pumble was one."

"She was?"

"Of course. Any brave, quick-thinking, free-spirited woman living in dark times is thought to be a witch—didn't you know that?"

The forest was so tightly packed with lush bamboo trees that Gertie couldn't even see the sky. It was such a change from the dry heat of North Africa, where she had helped return the measuring stick to Eratosthenes. Now it was a sword they had to give back, which they hoped would lead them to the B.D.B.U.

Gertie removed the weapon from its sheath.

"It's still glowing, but which way?"

"Oh, this is a nightmare," Kolt lamented. "I have no idea why the Losers would have brought the B.D.B.U. to ancient China and why the B.D.B.U. wanted us to bring along the very weapon capable of destroying it! We could be dealing with anything."

Then Robot Rabbit Boy pointed at a young bamboo tree.

"Lavender!" he cried.

"Yes," Kolt said. "I saw something, too. We may not be alone."

"Then I think we should get moving," suggested Gertie. "Anywhere is better than just standing here."

Without being asked, the newly appointed Keeper of Lost Things, Robot Rabbit Boy, bravely hopped out in front and began leading the charge, which would have appeared more heroic if Gertie hadn't had to keep lifting him over low bushes.

It was slow going through the dense undergrowth. The farther they went down the mountain, the more humid it got. Soon they were all drenched in sweat.

"If we don't find water," Kolt panted, "we might have to return to Skuldark."

"We can't do that," said Gertie. "We've come so far, and remember what you said about the Losers? The B.D.B.U. needs our help. Without it, I've got no chance of finding out who I am."

Kolt stopped walking and stood there.

"And if you did discover who you are, Gertie?" he asked indignantly. "What then? Would you leave us forever? What about your Keeper promise?"

"I haven't made any promises!" Gertie said crossly. "And

I failed my last mission, so I don't know why you'd want me to stay anyway."

They continued on in complete silence, broken only by the occasional offer of mashed potato.

But when something moved in the trees ahead, Kolt and Gertie exchanged a look that extinguished any tension between them.

"Who is there?" Kolt called out. "Show yourself! We are seekers of a giant book, and have a deadly rabbit."

"I'm not sure they speak our language."

"All Keepers speak Skuldarkian, Gertie, so anything we say translates into whichever language the listener best understands."

A man and a boy about Gertie's age stepped out from behind some bamboo trees, brandishing long staffs to defend themselves. They wore loose, light-brown robes of a cloth made from plant fibers.

"Hello!" said Kolt, placing his fist against an open palm and then bowing. The familiar greeting seemed to put the strangers at ease, and they returned the gesture. Then they spotted Robot Rabbit Boy's glowing eyes, and the older man stood in front of the boy, as if to shield him.

"Who are you people?"

"We are friends from very far away," Kolt said.

"Very, very far," added Gertie with a nod.

"From over the mountain?" the boy asked with excited curiosity. Then he turned to the older man. "Father, we've never been there, but you've told me many stories."

The father smiled at his son, then pointed his wooden staff at Robot Rabbit Boy, who was trying to copy Kolt by making a fist-paw and bowing.

Gertie tried not to laugh.

"Are you spirits?" the father said. "You look like foreigners but speak our language."

Kolt smiled. "Oh yes! We enjoy—"

"Listen! Please!" Gertie interrupted, remembering how serious their mission was. "We're in great danger and we need your help, now!"

Gertie reached for the sword and pulled the glittering weapon from its sheath. It was apparently the wrong thing to do as both the father and son fell to their knees at the shock of seeing it.

"Put that thing away!" Kolt hissed. "It must be some kind of talisman."

Gertie blushed. "I was hoping they might recognize it!"

"It's the lost sword of Mogan!" exclaimed the father.

Kolt scratched his chin. "Is that good or bad?

The father got up cautiously from the jungle floor and approached the sword.

"The shape is unmistakable, and the brightness of the metal and this silver writing on the blade. It is the sword of the legendary weapon-forging couple, Mo Ye and Gan Jiang, which means you are part of the prophecy."

"This mountain was named after them," the son said. "We call it *mo-gan-shan*."

"Great!" Kolt said. "A prophecy! Now we're making progress. Can you take us to them?"

"Please!" added Gertie. "They may be able to help us find something very, very valuable that we've lost."

The father and son looked at each other in amazement.

Finally the older man spoke. "They were killed many years ago by our king, who has brought great evil to this place."

Kolt rolled his eyes. "Oh dear, so not good news after all."

Then Gertie had an idea. "Did they have children?"

The son nodded. "They had a daughter, and she is still alive. We give her food sometimes, and can bring you to her home."

Kolt was impressed. "Good thinking, Gertie. You really are a first-rate Keeper of Lost Things!"

"Well, I don't feel like one," she replied. "Wearing denim in the jungle."

31

Bone Powder

THE FOREST GOT HOTTER and stickier as they stepped over gnarled tree roots along a narrow path, past small waterfalls that dropped into deep ponds. Gertie felt certain they were going the right way—but knew enough about being a Keeper to know that anything could happen, and to be on guard at all times.

Along the way, the father introduced himself as Li Dan. His son's name was Li Er.

Kolt explained to Gertie and Robot Rabbit Boy that in China, surnames come first, because the family is thought to be more important than the individual person.

Dan said he was a rice farmer. In the evening, when he came home, arms and legs aching, his son would make up simple and beautiful poems, as they all slurped river fish soup with lotus and ginger. By luck or coincidence, Dan and his son Er were two of the few people in the area who knew the sword makers' daughter well. She had spent most of her life in hiding from the evil king. For years, they had taken her cooked rice wrapped in leaves.

As they followed the forest trail toward the valley, Gertie listened to Er's stories. He explained that Chinese knowledge was not something to be accepted or rejected, but a wisdom that had to be lived.

"It is only understood when it becomes part of the seeker's destiny," he told her.

"What's it called?" Gertie asked.

"It has no name, it was never born and will never die."

The ideas rolled around Gertie's head like a bead from an abacus. "I'll think about it," she said.

Er laughed. "Oh Gertie, you must learn to do, by *not* doing."

Kolt happened to overhear the last sentence, as they descended slowly down some wet rocks. "Oh I'm great at that," he blurted out. "I've spent an entire lifetime perfecting the art of not doing!"

"I think what my son means," Dan said gently, "is that when something is from the heart, it doesn't feel like hard work."

When Er asked about Gertie's village, she told him it was near the sea, and there were large white birds and other creatures, tall cliffs with deep, dark tunnels, and friendly insects that lit up when you held them.

"I can't imagine," Er said. "If only I could see for myself."

Slowly, Gertie took the Slug Lamp from her pocket and

gave it to her friend to hold. The creature glowed brightly in Er's hands.

"Moonberries," Gertie said. "That's where they get their brightness."

Soon they came upon a hut made from straw and bamboo. Inside someone was shouting.

"You have to get out!"

Kolt caught Gertie's eye. "Sounds like the Losers have got here first!"

"Why won't you listen to me?" came the voice. "C'mon! Move! You won't survive here. Go back to your own kind!"

Before they could take cover behind some trees, a woman dashed outside with a grasshopper on her hand. She set the insect on the edge of a rock basin, which had been hollowed out and filled with water, to reflect the sky and passing clouds. "Rest here on the well of heaven!" she said. Then, turning sharply, she realized she had company.

The farmer and his son smiled and bowed. "It's us, Xiao Jian, your friends Dan and Er with visitors who have a gift."

Gertie unsheathed the ancient weapon, but, just as she gripped the hilt, it flew toward Xiao Jian, who caught it in both hands.

Kolt was completely amazed. "I guess it's hers then!"

When Xiao Jian saw the writing on the blade, Gertie noticed her hands were shaking. Then tears escaped from the woman's eyes, making her cheeks glisten.

"I don't think she has the B.D.B.U." Kolt sighed. "I'm not even sure it's here anymore."

"We can't just give up!"

Then Xiao Jian had something to say.

"For my entire life I have been waiting for the day this sword is returned so I can honor my ancestors and live out my destiny."

"The prophecy!" Dan said. "It is the will of heaven."

Then she turned to her visitors. "I will tell you my long and sad story over yellow tea and sweet bean cake."

Gertie was touched by the woman's show of emotion. For she had also felt the sting of loss, and knew that, on Skuldark, she would be living out a similar fate, lost from those she had loved. But there was no time for sentiment.

Gertie bowed to Xiao Jian. "Sorry we can't stay, but we're looking for a huge book that's very powerful. It was stolen, and we need to get it back."

The woman nodded. "There's only one person I know who would crave such a powerful thing, and my destiny lies with him too."

"Oh no," said Kolt. "It's going to be some crazy evil person, I just know it."

"A ruthless king," said the woman. "The one who killed my parents and opposes all knowledge. He is famous in our land for his destruction of ideas, and the torture of his people within the deadly Crown of Triangles."

"Hates knowledge? Destruction of ideas? Crown of deadly shapes?" Kolt said. "Definitely sounds like someone the Losers would be friends with."

"Can we go there now?" Gertie asked.

Then Dan spoke. "There is a *knowledge sacrifice* planned for this very night, which I fear will involve the destruction of wisdom in your lost book."

"A what?" Kolt said.

"An evening where the king destroys any idea he does not agree with," Er said.

Xiao Jian tied the sword around her waist with a length of black silk. "We must leave immediately, as it will take time to reach the village through such thick forest."

"Then let's get moving!" Gertie said, with a renewed sense of hope.

Suddenly, an enormous dark shape thundered toward them from the dense undergrowth. Everyone jumped back at the sound of sticks and branches snapping in the charge. Xiao Jian drew her sword, but it turned out to be Robot Rabbit Boy riding on the back of a full-grown water buffalo.

"Mashed potato! Dollop! Eggcup!" he commanded, and the animal stopped just shy of trampling the farmer and his son. The water buffalo snorted and rolled its eyes lovingly at his rabbit driver.

Er patted the creature's head. "It is in winter that pine trees are their greenest."

"What?" said Kolt. "I thought pine trees were always green!"

"My son means that friendship and loyalty count most in hard times when others shy away."

With Robot Rabbit Boy leading the charge, they descended in a single line behind the water buffalo who stampeded through the undergrowth.

"I'm sorry about your parents," Gertie said moving up alongside Xiao Jian. "I know how it feels to lose family."

"You have brought honor to my family, Gertie, by returning this sword."

"What exactly happened to them?"

"My parents were famous sword makers," Xiao Jian explained, "with a special way of hardening metal by cooling it in the mountain waters. No one could rival the sharp edges or decoration. The new king ordered a sword to be made in three months. But it took my parents three years because they wanted to please him, despite his growing reputation for cruelty.

"They made two weapons, a female and a male sword. The first they gave him, the second they hid for me when I was older.

"I was only eight years old when they went down the mountain to present the female sword to our king. It was supposed to have been an exciting day since the king had said my family would receive a great reward for such loyalty. My father wanted me to come, but my mother was worried about the king's rumored temper and insisted I stay.

"I waited many days for them to return, dreaming of riches and fame. Our neighbors brought me food and made sure I was safe and that my fire was out by the evening bell.

"When they did not return for four days, I was worried and followed the forest path by myself to get news. When people found out who I was, they turned away."

"Why?" Gertie said, as Kolt caught up so he could hear the story too.

"Because they were scared. The young, angry king was insulted he had not been given both swords. The thought of someone else having such a magnificent weapon filled him with jealousy. So he took the female sword and cut my parents' heads off. Then he boiled their heads and crushed the bones into a powder, which he put around his neck in a bottle."

Kolt grimaced. "Please don't tell me this is the king we're on our way to meet? I'm fine with most things, but head-boiling is way out of my comfort zone."

"Now I intend to get back the bones of my parents by any means necessary."

Gertie looked at the weapon in Xiao Jian's hands. "And so I guess this is the male sword?"

The woman nodded. "The king sent soldiers to kill me and retrieve the male weapon, but nobody knew where it was hidden. My parents' friends heard what was happening and carried me up the mountain, where they sheltered and fed me until I could look after myself. I have been in hiding ever since, every day searching the jungle for the lost sword of Mogan."

"So what's the prophecy?" Kolt asked.

"That the sword of Mo and Gan will be reunited with its

rightful owner, who will bring peace to a land that has only known terror."

"I guess that means you," Kolt said. "This is turning into some kind of quest! I love it!"

When the air picked up an aroma of wood smoke, Xiao Jian said they were near. The path began to even out, and they were soon standing on a flat plain, at the base of the green mountain. Ahead of them in the distance were the walls of the town, where the evil king reigned.

After hurrying over the grassy savanna, they approached the heavy door. Gertie stepped forward and banged on it several times. A hatch decorated with a triangle and snake opened to reveal a pair of eyes.

"It's almost nightfall and we have a sacrifice to get through," said a voice. "You know the rules, go away."

"Er," Gertie stammered. "We're looking for a giant book."

The eyes blinked with confusion. "A giant book?"

"Actually," Kolt interrupted, "I forgot my hat in there earlier, mind if we come in quickly and look for it?"

"Your hat? I don't remember you. Where did you leave it?"

"In a bucket!" cried Gertie impulsively.

The eyes widened with surprise and irritation. "You forgot your hat in a bucket?"

Then Xiao Jian marched forward and put her face to the hatch. "We have come to fulfill the will of heaven and reunite the male and female swords of Mo and Gan!"

The eyes shot open with fear and disbelief. "But that's a fairy story—the male sword doesn't exist. . . ."

Xiao Jian held up her gleaming weapon.

"Oh," said the eyes. "So it does exist."

The hatch closed, and they heard bolts shifting inside the wood.

Robot Rabbit Boy kissed the water buffalo's veiny cheek, then slid down off the enormous animal.

The doorkeeper was an old man with a bent back.

"You should have just said you were here to fulfill a prophecy! How was I supposed to know?"

Gertie was surprised to see the town was mostly small wooden huts with dried leaves for roofs. A temple at the end of the main path was bigger and more imposing than anything around it. Dan and Er said it was the king's palace. On the roof sat an enormous metal triangle with a wooden snake statue.

"It's the dreaded Crown of Triangles," Dan said fearfully. "Anyone who enters the king's chamber of horror is never seen again."

"I always disliked geometry," Kolt admitted. "And that was without snakes."

The idea of facing an evil king who had murdered people made Gertie feel very afraid. She wondered if allowing herself to become a Keeper had been wise. If anything happened to her, what would become of Robot Rabbit Boy and the Slug Lamp snoozing away in her pocket? She distracted herself by looking at the different things for sale in the market stalls; rolls of cloth, pottery, rings of precious jade, bronze cooking pots, sitting mats, chopsticks, and bamboo water flasks with smaller pieces of bamboo hollowed out as cups.

Much to Robot Rabbit Boy's delight, there were animals everywhere: sheep, chickens, pigs, Mongolian ponies, and his beloved water buffalos.

By now it was evening, and many of the market people were drinking hot water boiled with tree bark. But at the sight of Xiao Jian, Kolt, Gertie, Li Dan, Li Er, and Robot Rabbit Boy, the townsfolk stopped what they were doing and stared.

"They must know!" Gertie said. "That Xiao Jian has come to reunite the swords of her parents."

"That's *her* mission," Kolt told Gertie. "Ours is to find the B.D.B.U. then get out of here!"

"What about the Losers? Have you faced them before like this?"

"Not exactly," Kolt said.

"Well, do we have any weapons?"

"I might have some growing spice in my pocket, but then again, it might be shrinking spice. Did you bring anything?"

"Just a Slug Lamp and that feather I got in London."

"Oh dear, well, let's hope Xiao Jian takes care of the head-boiling king and his Loser friends, while we find the B.D.B.U."

"I *know* we can do this," Gertie said, wiping sweat and dust from her forehead. "I know we can."

"We have to, Gertie. Because if the B.D.B.U. dies, then so too may its Keepers."

32

The Final Fight

GERTIE DID NOT FEEL LIKE A HERO. Her legs trembled, and her heart pounded with such force it was difficult to breathe. Worst of all, a large group of local people were now following them, expecting some kind of death match between Gertie's group and the evil king.

"They think we're here to save them," Dan explained. "They have lived too long with a cruel and merciless king."

"Us?" Kolt said. "We're just Keepers, not assassins—can you tell them that? They'll believe you!"

But when the farmer explained to the crowd that Kolt, Gertie, and Robot Rabbit Boy were *not* deadly assassins, the people laughed and said that only deadly assassins would pretend not to be a group of deadly assassins.

Robot Rabbit Boy tugged on Gertie's sleeve as they neared the evil king's palace.

"A dollop of mashed potato?" he said, twitching his nose, as he had moments before blowing a hole in the trapdoor.

"Um, not right now! But maybe later, like when we're about to get our heads boiled...."

"Eggcup."

Suddenly a group of boyish soldiers rushed toward them with swords out. But Gertie didn't think they looked very fierce, with metal acorn helmets that kept falling over their eyes.

Xiao Jian spoke savagely as they approached. "I have come for the bones of my mother and father, so that I might honor them—beware those who defy what is mandated by heaven!"

Gertie thought the soldiers were going to surround them, so she grabbed Robot Rabbit Boy's paw, ready to sprint toward the village huts. But the guards seemed almost hypnotized by the weapon in Xiao Jian's hands, and parted without any resistance.

"I wonder why they're doing this?" Kolt whispered to Gertie.

"Because of the story?"

"Yes, exactly," Er interrupted. "The prophecy that one day the male and female swords would reunite to defeat the king and bring harmony back to the land."

"Oh right," Kolt said. "That makes sense. Man sword, woman sword equals harmony baby."

"Eggcup?"

"No, no, no," Kolt said. "Listen, Chinese wisdom has

three paths: Lao-tzu came first and wanted people to live in harmony with nature, then Confucius taught people to live in harmony with one another, then about four hundred years later, Buddha's ideas came from India and taught people how to live in harmony with themselves. Three paths to wisdom! Harmony, baby!"

"Mashed potato?"

When they arrived at the palace, it was nothing more than an oversize clay building with wooden windows cut into complicated geometric shapes. Painted on red panels were more triangles and snakes.

The soldiers who had let them pass were now chattering nervously with the villagers.

"More creepy snake drawings," Kolt said.

Gertie touched one. "Like Doll Head!" she pointed out. "I suppose if you make people afraid, they are easier to control."

Suddenly, two men in blue cloaks appeared from inside the palace doors.

"I am the minister for the sacrifice of birds," one of them said, bowing.

"And I am the minister for the sacrifice of the spotted deer," said the other, with an even lower bow.

Kolt stepped forward. "And we are ministers for the rescue of books."

The ministers explained that the king was expecting them and had prepared a feast in their honor. Kolt thought that sounded promising, but everyone else looked worried. They followed the two ministers through darkened rooms of the palace to a banquet hall with drums carved into wooden pillars that held up the roof.

On a low table, a lavish feast had been laid out, and there were mats on the floor for people to sit.

"Look at all that food!" Kolt said. "But I don't see the B.D.B.U. anywhere."

There were bronze vessels and ceramic bowls filled with sizzling dishes and, beside each dish, a set of silver chopsticks.

"Amazing! We must be in the Autumn and Spring time period of Zhou Dynasty," Kolt said. "About 600 B.C.E., just before China's descent into an epoch of warring states."

"What's an epoch?" Gertie asked.

"It means 'time period'—but I always thought using the same word twice in a phrase sounded bad."

"How do you know what epoch this is?"

"Well, for one, I saw soldiers with crossbows outside, and these dishes are typical. . . ." Kolt went on. "Stir-fried turtle with plum, snake and chestnuts, sizzling chicken with ginger and peach, wild dates with boiled snake. . . ."

Gertie looked over the steaming plates. "At least there are no heads."

Kolt chuckled. "We don't know what's for dessert yet."

"But why are the chopsticks silver?"

"Because people thought they would change color when touching poison."

"Then it's obvious," Gertie said. "If the king is worried about being poisoned—then he's most likely evil."

When something on one of the plates began to wriggle, Gertie felt fear seize her body. "I think it's a trap, Kolt. They know who we are, and the king is mostly likely preparing himself personally for battle with Xiao Jian."

"Gertie is right," Dan told them. "The feast is to honor us—a last meal. The king knows we are here and has planned for our execution during the knowledge sacrifice."

"Last meal!" Kolt said. "But I can't eat any of that, it's meat!"

Xiao Jian unsheathed her sword and readied herself for the arrival of the man who had killed her parents.

But Er, the farmer's son, had something to say. "Please, Xiao Jian, remember that water is soft but passes through mountains with no effort. This is why softness will always overcome hardness."

"He killed my family," Xiao Jian said bitterly. "I will do what I must."

Just then, attendants in brown cloaks appeared and began to beat the wooden pillar drums. Villagers crowded around the building and stared in through every lattice window.

"Oh dear," Kolt said. "Let's hope that's not the boiling song."

The drums got faster and faster, until the whole building began to shake. Then two doors opened to reveal a stocky man with a coarse beard and fierce eyes. His black hair was tied up into a triangular knot and pierced with a hair stick shaped like a snake.

With a roar of anger, he somersaulted into the main room, landing heavily at the front of the buffet table where he split a melon and a ceramic bowl with one downward swipe of his razor-sharp sword.

His eyes blazed as he glared at the uninvited guests. "You dare come here and challenge the king!"

Nobody spoke.

"Must be a rhetorical question," Kolt whispered.

Then Gertie noticed an oddly dressed boy and girl, about her age, enter quietly from the same door as the king.

"Who are they?" Gertie said, pointing them out to Kolt. "Definitely not locals by the look of them."

"Losers!" Kolt said. "And they knew we were coming, because they probably needed the other sword to destroy the B.D.B.U.! This sort of brilliant plan could only have been carried out by Thrax and conceived by Vispoth."

"But why would the B.D.B.U. allow us to bring it then?"

"I have no idea."

"Unless it was the only possible way we might rescue it?"

Gertie stared at the Losers, wondering what they were like and how they had come to join such a terrible gang of troublemakers. The girl especially filled Gertie with fascination. She was wearing a silver space suit and white hat made from thin metal that covered one side of her face and flashed with yellow lights. Was she, too, separated from her family?

The boy made her feel another way completely. He had on black pants and a black hooded sweater. His hair was short and combed neatly to one side. It was as though she had seen him before, but couldn't remember where. Gertie searched the darkness in her mind for a single detail, a feeling, the sound of his voice, a word—anything that would give meaning to the strange way she was feeling.

When the boy noticed Kolt and Gertie staring at him, he whispered something to the girl, and she sneered. Then he looked straight at Gertie and grinned.

Before Gertie could ask Kolt why the Losers were smiling at her, a group of sixteen soldiers carried in a wooden table, upon which the B.D.B.U. sat open, but lifeless.

The king raised his sword and took aim at the giant book.

"Glad you could make it!" the Loser boy with neat hair suddenly shouted toward Kolt. "You're just in time to see this stupid old book get chopped to nothing."

His words were angry and sharp, like scissors cutting through the sentence. The girl in the space suit popped the gum she was chewing.

"Yeah," she said. "Destroyed forever!"

Kolt glared at them. "You fools, give us that book back immediately. It doesn't belong to you."

"Seriously?" Gertie said. "That's your argument? What's the backup plan?"

"Backup plan? I don't think we even had a *plan*."

But then Xiao Jian marched right up to the king with her sword out.

"You dare!" he cried, raising the fabled female weapon over his head. Gertie could see the fear in his eyes, and it reassured her there was a chance they would win and get the B.D.B.U. back.

"You have the bones of my parents around your neck," Xiao Jian said with a calmness that impressed everyone.

The Losers did not seem pleased. "You promised an old woman would bring the male sword to us!" the boy said ferociously. "But you didn't mention that she was an assassin!"

"I'm not just any assassin!" roared Xiao Jian. "I am the daughter of Mo Ye and Gan Jiang!"

The villagers and guards crowded in at the windows and doorways, not wanting to miss a single word.

"So you've come for your parents' bones?" The king laughed. "I will trade them for the sword you carry."

With everyone's attention on the two swords, Gertie nudged Robot Rabbit Boy, and the two of them crept toward the table with the B.D.B.U.

When the Loser boy noticed Gertie and her robot companion sneaking across the banquet hall, he didn't make any attempt to stop them but smiled again, as though he were on her side and this was all part of some plan.

Gertie was almost there when the king backflipped so that he was standing on the B.D.B.U. with his sword ready.

"I shall destroy this book first with my sword, then take yours to complete the job!" he said, spitting the words rather than saying them. "After I've thrown you all into the Crown of Triangles."

The villagers and guards gasped with horror.

But just as he was about to skewer the ancient volume with his magical steel blade, Xiao Jian's body flew through the air like a dart, and the swords of male and female clashed in a shower of white sparks.

The final battle had begun.

33

The Ultimate Sacrifice

THE PATH TO THE B.D.B.U. was now blocked by the ferocious sword fight and aerial acrobatics of the king and Xiao Jian. Even if Gertie had been able to dive for the old book, there was no way she could have lifted it without the help of at least ten villagers.

Everyone looked on, hardly able to breathe, as the king and Xiao Jian somersaulted around the room, swords clashing and legs flying up into twisting kicks. Kolt, Gertie, and Robot Rabbit Boy took cover under the banquet table.

"It's right there!" Gertie cried. "We're so close—all we need is to touch it, link up, and put the key in the lock."

"They're moving too quickly," Kolt pointed out. "If we get in the way we'll be cut to ribbons."

Just then the king's sword missed Xiao Jian's head by

an inch, and struck a beam, showering everyone with splinters of wood.

"I'm going over there," Gertie said impulsively. "Join me when you can and we'll get out of here!" Before Kolt could stop her, she jumped out from under the table and made a run for the B.D.B.U. The evil king saw, and, while defending against a side blow from Xiao Jian's glimmering blade, grabbed a wooden bowl and hurled it at Gertie, hitting her square in the nose.

She fell to the floor, hands over her face. Kolt and Robot Rabbit Boy leapt out from under the table and pulled her to safety.

"What are you doing?" Kolt said. "Trying to get yourself killed?"

"I thought I saw a chance," Gertie said, her nose throbbing. "I had no idea he'd throw a stupid bowl!"

"He boils people's heads, Gertie! What did you expect? And we *all* need to be touching before I turn my key in the time machine."

At that moment, the king struck Xiao Jian's sword with such force that the ancient weapon flew from her hand and stuck in the table next to where the farmer's son, Li Er, was hiding.

The boy got up and looked at Xiao Jian's male sword, still quivering where it had stuck the wood.

The king laughed heartily. "What are you going to do child? Grab Xiao Jian's sword and fight me with it yourself?"

Seeing that Xiao Jian was defeated, the villagers felt afraid, and the terrified guards laughed along with their evil master as he stood ridiculing Li Er, his own sword hovering at Xiao Jian's throat.

But Er did not seem angry or afraid, and he spoke to the king in the gentle way he had spoken with Gertie as they came down the mountain.

"I don't need this sword to defeat you." He smiled. "I have a more powerful weapon...."

"You'll pay for that arrogance!" the king cried. He summoned his fearful guards to watch the now-swordless Xiao Jian, and started toward Er. The villagers screamed. The farmer rushed to protect his son, but Er told his father he was in no danger.

"No danger?" the king growled, advancing closer.

"None at all," Er said, winking at Gertie. "For the great weapon I will use to defeat you was something I found on my way here, a *soft*, bright force that is stronger than mountains."

"And what is that?" the king cried. "A poison-tipped qiang spear? A fu ax? Crossbow? Throwing daggers?"

"No." Er smiled. "My weapon is friendship."

Then he looked right at Gertie and winked again.

Finally she understood what he was getting at, and, as the enraged king stormed up to Er, Gertie silently tipped an enormous jug of water onto its side, sending a slick torrent across the stone. But the stone floor was not level, and, to Gertie's horror, the path of the water suddenly changed course, causing the mini flood to rush behind where the king was walking.

The evil king laughed. "You think you can stop a great warrior with water?" he snorted. "There is nothing *soft* that could ever hurt me!"

What happened next caught everyone by surprise and would be recorded in the history books for eternity.

A small, *soft*, squishy thing shot like a bullet from Gertie's pocket, so that when the king brought his foot down he slipped onto his back, banging his head and knocking himself out cold—right next to the squished blob that had once lived happily under the moonberry bush outside the Keepers' cottage, completely unaware of its fate to one day save the human race.

The villagers, maids, guards, attendants, and even the soldiers went mad with cheers and clapping. It was the bravest, most daring sacrifice ever made in the history of Slug Lamp kind.

With a mixture of anger, sorrow, and pride, Gertie grabbed the king's sword from the stone floor and ran over to the Losers, who all this time had just been standing there like a pair of idiots.

"Surrender!" she cried. "You've lost."

But they just stared at her with no emotion. Gertie couldn't figure it out. She didn't like how calm they seemed, as though everything had been rehearsed and they were just waiting for the scene to play itself out.

"Stay where you are!" she ordered. "Don't try to escape."

The Loser boy just laughed.

Suddenly, there was a loud wail. The king had come around and was screaming for mercy. "Don't kill me, please, please!" he pleaded as Xiao Jian stood over him with a dagger she been given by one of the king's soldiers.

She was red with fury. "You murdered my parents and killed many of your own people."

Gertie could feel the pain in her voice. It filled the hearts of everyone listening. Then she remembered some wisdom Er had shared with her on their walk down the mountain, and it suddenly made sense.

"Xiao Jian!" Gertie called from across the hall. "You must spare the king's life. If you kill him, a part of you will also die."

Xiao Jian let out a piercing cry, hoisted the dagger high in the air, and swung it fiercely over the king's neck, cutting the string that held the glass bottle with her parents' ground-up bones.

Xiao Jian stood strong and tall over the man who had spent his life bringing terror and sadness to everyone he met. The villagers escorted their old leader to a jail cell.

"Great speech," Kolt said. "Very wise words."

"I was just repeating what the farmer's son told me on our walk down the mountain."

"The farmer's son?"

"Yes," said Gertie, looking for his face in the crowd, "the boy called Li Er."

"Li Er?" Kolt said. "Why didn't I realize it before? That's Lao-tzu! China's first major philosopher!"

The Loser boy who had been observing all this cleared his throat. "Have you finished jabbering?" he said. "Because Gertie and I have a book to destroy."

Gertie held the sword up. "I'm not falling for your dumb tricks." She looked to Kolt for advice. "Let's take them to the beach for Johnny the Guard Worm."

"Well . . . I wouldn't sleep knowing they were down there with the innocent dodos. Let's leave them here in jail with the evil king—though they'll eventually get picked up by their Loser friends in Doll Head, if it's not already on its way."

"But Gertie," the boy said, "you don't need to pretend anymore, we've done it! Let's follow through with Thrax's plan and get out of here."

Gertie stared blankly at him, trying to untangle his words into something she understood.

"She really has lost her whole memory!" the Loser girl with the white metal hat said. "Sewing her name on the gown didn't do any good."

Gertie gasped and took a step back.

"Oh dear," Kolt said under his breath. "Oh dearie dear . . ."

Gertie felt her blood turn ice cold. "It must be a trick. Maybe they saw the gown in my bedroom when they broke into the cottage."

"Impossible. They couldn't get into any of the rooms, remember?"

"You're going to have to tell her," the girl said to the boy with black hair. "Like Thrax said you would."

"Tell me what!"

"You might not want to know," Kolt warned her. "Might be better to just leave. . . all we need to do is stand on the table with the B.D.B.U. and link up."

"Shut up, old man!" the Loser girl snapped. "You're not taking that book anywhere. Gertie, go get the other sword so we can spike this oversize comic."

But Gertie was frozen to the spot with emotions blazing inside her. The Loser boy stepped forward, completely ignoring the sword in her hand.

"You've done it," he said. "Don't you understand? The plan worked. We've won. You're a hero."

34

The Crown of Triangles

GERTIE HAD THE MOST horrible sick feeling in her stomach.

"Stay back," she snarled, raising her sword at the boy. "I'm not afraid to use this on you!"

"Listen," he said, "you've lost your memory. So *listen*, because I'm going to remind you what happened during the Information War to our—"

"Ignore them!" yelled Kolt. "He's just stalling until reinforcements arrive! Let's go!"

"You're from Los Angeles!" cried the boy.

"What? How do you know that?"

"Because I'm your brother, Gertie—we were rescued by Cava Calla Thrax after our parents were arrested for reading illegal books to us."

"Stop!" Gertie said. "Don't say any more, you're not my

family, I'm going to find my real family, you don't know anything about them."

"Gertie!" Kolt said.

"Shut up, you old git!" snarled the girl. "Keeper scum!"

The boy continued to talk. "The Library Police tried to defend them, but the government took our mom and dad away, and we were left in the ruined city to fend for ourselves. . . . I have your diaries to prove it!"

"Where are they then?"

"At base camp with Thrax, Gertie. The Losers gave us food, shelter, and the promise of a peaceful life in return for one favor, just one tiny thing—to help steal an old book and destroy it."

"My parents are alive? Where are they?"

"That's all we had to do, that's all Thrax and the Losers wanted: get that other sword and destroy the book once and for all, for if humans lived in ignorance, there would be no Information War, and—"

"Stop!" Gertie cried, advancing with her weapon until it was inches from the boy's neck. "Stop lying to me!"

Just then, there was a deep rumbling, and outside they heard screaming.

The Loser girl laughed. "Peasant fools!" she said. "I'd like to see their faces now."

"It's Doll Head!" shouted Kolt. "Gertie, we have to go!"

But Gertie was still trying to wrestle truth from what the boy was saying.

"Then how did you get me to Skuldark? Only true Keepers can do that."

Doll Head swooped down so low that piercing light from its eye sockets swept over the banquet hall, blinding everyone long enough for the Loser boy to turn and run. Gertie dropped the sword and gave chase.

"Gertie!" screamed Kolt. "Gertie, come back! Let him go!"

But she had to know. She had to learn the truth about who she was, even if it meant failing the mission.

Gertie sprinted after him through the palace, their footsteps echoing over the plank floors.

"Stop!" Gertie cried. "Wait!"

Suddenly, they came upon the golden statue of a snake and triangle. As the Loser boy scooted past, the snake's eyes opened, and an enormous triangular door in the floor flipped up. The boy disappeared through it. Gertie bit her lip and slid down into the darkness after him, the trapdoor slamming shut behind her.

When she opened her eyes and sat up, she was surrounded by dozens of other Gertie Milks. She blinked hard in the milky light and realized she was in a hall of mirrors, where each face was a reflection in a polished triangle of rock.

"It's the Crown of Triangles," whimpered the boy's voice. "The king told us about it, and there's no escape."

"Where are you?" Gertie said, noticing his face in several of the rock mirrors. "And what's with all these weird reflections?"

"It's a pit," said the boy, his voice trembling. "The Crown of Triangles is a snake pit. It's where the king put his enemies to die."

Gertie looked down at her feet but saw only the shadow of her shoes in the dirt.

"I don't see any snakes."

"They're coming. . . ."

"Then we have to get out!"

"There's no way!" said the boy. "The king said it was impossible."

"Where are you anyway?" Gertie said, moving slowly through the maze of mirrored rocks. Then she saw his face, but when she approached, she realized it was just another reflection.

"I can see you!" cried the boy, "But I can't find you."

"It's a hall of mirrors," Gertie said. "Stay calm. It's meant to frighten, like that idiotic doll head you fly around in."

Then Gertie saw something move. Her heart was pumping fast, but she knew if she panicked now, she would have no chance to get away.

"Where are you?" screamed the boy. "Gertie! There's something moving."

Gertie turned in all directions, seeing the boy's distress reflected in every rock mirror.

"If we're going to die," Gertie said, "you may as well tell me the truth: if *I am* your sister, and a Loser, then how did you get me to Skuldark with a Keeper's key?"

"B-b-because you *are* a Keeper," the boy said fearfully.

"A real Keeper! And the Losers knew you would eventually be sent to Skuldark, which is why your gown had tracking chips sewn into it. It was my idea to put your name on the outside, just in case you lost your memory—which is what Thrax said must happen to new Keepers, in order for them to fulfill their duties and accept their new lives."

"I was chosen?"

"No, you were stolen from your life, as all Keepers are, Gertie—the B.D.B.U. is not your friend, it kidnapped aaarrgh!"

"What is it?"

"A snake! I just touched a snake!"

Gertie heard shuffling, and then a heavy thud.

"What happened? Are you all right?"

"My head," the boy whimpered. "I'm bleeding. I ran into the rock, and now I feel . . ." His voice trailed off.

"Hey!" Gertie cried. "I'll find you. . . . Hang in there."

"Trapped forever," he mumbled. "We'll never escape."

Gertie was about to ask another question when the boy said something that made her think everything he'd told her was true.

"At least we'll die together, Gertie, as we always thought we would, back in the ruined city."

Gertie swam frantically through the dim light, feeling her way beyond the many versions of herself that were not real. Eventually she found her brother, curled up on the floor, blood leaking from a gash in his head.

"Get up!" she screamed, noticing a dark line curl silently toward him. "Snake!"

With a shriek, he leapt up off the ground and into her arms.

"Help!" he wailed, trying to choke back tears of terror.

Gertie steadied him by the shoulders, then couldn't stop herself and pulled the boy into a tight hug.

"I hate snakes," he sobbed.

"Then why did you choose to visit an evil king who keeps them as pets, you idiot?"

"It was Thrax's idea," the boy said, breaking the embrace. "Based on Vispoth's calculations. There are chemicals in the two swords that react to something in the B.D.B.U., creating an explosion big enough to incinerate it."

"Sounds like you were intended to be part of the sacrifice."

"Thrax wouldn't do that. . . . He would have rescued us again, he's a—"

". . . terrifying, evil, time-traveling Roman who destroys knowledge and murders people with the help of a totally insane supercomputer that makes hot chocolate?"

"All I know," the boy said, "is that he saved us, Gertie, just like you saved me by jumping down into the Crown of Triangles."

"But don't you understand?" Gertie implored him. "We *can't* destroy the book! I'll die! The human race will be doomed."

"It doesn't matter now," said the boy. "That one snake has probably gone to get the others—or some kind of snake king."

"Or queen . . ." Gertie said. "Like bees."

With the boy's arm around her shoulder, they edged through the rock-mirror maze, looking for some form of escape.

"So I'm really a Keeper?" Gertie asked.

"*Yes,* and you were supposed to steal the B.D.B.U. and that sword while Kolt was broken down in the dinosaur apple orchard. That's why we were there in Doll Head—to pick you up. We sabotaged the Time Cat in Alexandria so that it would break down and you'd have a chance to be in the cottage by yourself, but *you* forgot, because you lost your memory, and so we had to do it by following the tracking beacon we had sewn into your gown, which was made to look like a rag."

"I don't even know your name," Gertie said, stopping to catch her breath.

"You do," said the boy. "You just forgot it."

"Tell me."

"Gareth Milk."

"I had a feeling you knew me," she confessed. "Because you didn't stare at my birthmark, which means you were used to it."

"So you believe me?"

"I think so."

"About everything?"

"Yes, but it doesn't matter if we can't find our way out of this place."

Gertie was just about to mention how surprising it was there were so few snakes—given how many snake signs there were in the village—when they turned into a room that was literally littered with human skeletons.

Silky black creatures wriggled through the fleshless white bones.

Gareth held on to his sister, too terrified to even scream.

"I guess this is the cafeteria," Gertie said, surprised by her calm toughness. Then the longest, fattest, most terrifying snake in the room released an almost-meatless skeleton and slithered toward them.

Gertie grabbed hold of her brother and began to backtrack.

"Don't look!" she cried. "Just keep moving."

For what seemed like an eternity, they sidestepped, shuffled, and shimmied through the deadly Crown of Triangles, where everything and nothing were real.

"Here!" Gareth called, feeling a space between two polished rock mirrors. It was a small chamber and they crawled in.

"Let's stay in here for now," Gertie said, hoping that Kolt and Robot Rabbit Boy were looking for them and not still ogling the buffet table. The cramped space was so dark, it was the first time since falling into the evil king's dungeon they could no longer see themselves, or any versions of themselves.

"We're just voices now," Gareth said somberly. "Like we're losing ourselves piece by piece."

"Tell me something. . . ." Gertie whispered.

"What?"

"How did you get into the tower with the B.D.B.U.? Your stolen Keeper's key didn't work on any of the other doors."

"We took imprints of your hands before you departed for Skuldark, just in case you forgot what you were supposed to do."

"So I guess I really am a Loser?"

"Through and through."

Gertie felt dizzy, as though her thoughts were being pulled apart. This boy, her brother, had to be right. It all made sense. Even Johnny the Guard Worm, she realized, was trained only to catch Losers.

"Hey!" Gareth said, taking Gertie's hand and rubbing it on the ground. "The earth here is soft!"

"You're right!" she said, digging her fingers into it.

As they clawed at the loose dirt, Gareth confessed to Gertie how much he had missed her, and how he had told the Losers so many stories about their lives growing up together in Los Angeles before the Information War.

"I knew you'd remember me sometime," he said.

"I don't remember you! And I'm still confused about everything."

"Well, ask me anything. I'll help you find your memories."

Gertie wanted to ask what she was like before her trip to Skuldark. But part of her was afraid to know. Then she remembered what Kolt had told her about Mrs. Pumble putting truth spice in a Loser's moonberry juice, and although it made her feel guilty, and sly, and disloyal, she decided to ask her brother something that might help the Keeper cause.

"How did Thrax know I was a Keeper before I disappeared?" she said, turning to check they were still alone. "How do the Losers know which children are going to be called to Skuldark?"

"That's simple! Vispoth analyzes missing children lists. And so it's just a matter of going to the point in time when the child goes missing. . . . Those who disappear in a flash of orange light are Keepers."

"So why are there so few of them on Skuldark?"

"Because," Gertie's brother boasted, "the Losers have been traveling through time and kidnapping them before they disappear, hiding them in towers, dungeons, jails, and on snow-capped mountains!"

"But wouldn't they just disappear anyway?" Gertie said. "It's fated to happen. . . ."

The boy laughed. "Not with the magnetic cuff we slap on their wrists."

Gertie remembered what Kolt had told her about staying away from magnets.

"So all the Keepers who should be on Skuldark helping return lost things," the boy went on proudly, "are rotting away in prisons throughout time where no one can find them!"

"And you think that's good!" Gertie hissed. "It's the most horrible, evil thing I've ever heard! If we both die in here, it serves us right!"

"You don't know what you're saying, Gertie. . . . Cava Calla Thrax came for us, he helped us! When we were alone and starving during the worst, most violent years of the Information War!"

"He *used* us, more like," Gertie said. "If I wasn't fated to be a Keeper, he'd never have come for us, you must know that."

"So what?" said her brother, beginning to lose his temper. "He helped us, so we could help him—it's what happens in a family."

"A family of psychos!" Gertie said with a long sigh. "Just keep digging!"

After several more handfuls, a powerful line of white light lit up the small chamber of rock they had squeezed into.

"That's it!" Gareth exclaimed. "It must be outside! Help! Help!"

"Shut up!" Gertie barked, pushing him away from the crack. "If the snake finds us, we're done for!"

"But I hear voices," Gareth said, laying his ear flat against the stone, "like someone is saying 'eggcup' over and over again."

35

The Meaning of Loyalty

GERTIE RIPPED A BUTTON from her sleeve and shoved it through the hole. "Keep listening!" she told her brother.

Then from behind came the stench of foul, rotting air, and the grating sweep of scales dragged over dirt.

"Oh no," Gertie said.

Gareth still had his ear to the cold stone. "What's so special about the little x below a rabbit's nose?"

Gertie realized what was about to happen and grabbed her Loser brother, pulling him out of the chamber and back into the Crown of Triangles where they came face-to-face with the giant maze snake.

"What are you doing?" Gareth cried. "Are you mad? It's right there?"

The snake stared at the boy and girl, its forked tongue pulsing in and out of its mouth.

C'mon... Gertie thought, waiting for the thunder of an explosion that would mean they were free, *do it*... but nothing was happening.

Then suddenly she remembered something Kolt had told her about Johnny the Guard Worm, and had an idea. As the snake slithered toward them, Gertie pulled out the peacock feather her friend had given her in London, and began waving it in the air. The snake stopped, entranced by the dazzling blue eye and shimmering green.

Then she stepped toward the enormous serpent and swept the peacock feather gently over the snake's scales.

Her Loser brother stood paralyzed as Gertie tickled the deadliest jewel in the Crown of Triangles. After a moment the black snake rolled onto its back, so that Gertie could tickle its belly.

"So much for the Crown of Triangles," Gertie said, as a massive laser blast tore open the rock wall of the nearby chamber. The snake pulled back in fright and retreated to its lair. Gertie put the feather back in her pocket, grabbed her Loser brother, and ran through the dust and over the pile of rubble.

Robot Rabbit Boy was so happy to see them, he jumped into Gertie's arms with such force that he knocked her and Gareth Milk to the ground.

"Thank goodness you're alive," Kolt said. "The Loser girl escaped into her ship, just in case you were wondering what happened to the—"

Gareth jumped to his feet. "C'mon, Gertie, forget the rabbit and the old man—let's destroy that book!"

They were out in the open, somewhere near the palace. In the distance, the Losers' ship was hovering over the villagers who were dashing about with spears and swords, perhaps wondering why the prophecy hadn't mentioned flying doll heads.

Gertie couldn't believe what she was hearing. "Didn't you learn anything about me in that weird snake mirror place?"

Her brother was amazed. "You said you believed me!"

"I do believe you, but I've changed, Gareth. Maybe it was losing my memory of the Information War that did it, but I don't believe in destroying things now, I believe in returning them to the world. Don't you see? It's not the knowledge that matters, but what people can do with it, the hope it gives them . . . that's what counts."

"But I'm your family, Gertie! Your brother, we're Losers."

Doll Head swooped viciously over where they were standing, its engines whirring.

"I know!" Gertie said, looking at Kolt and Robot Rabbit Boy. "I want to come with you, I really do, but—"

"You're not the sister I grew up with!" he growled.

"Well, it's who I am now!" Gertie said, defending herself, "which is why I can't go with you, and why I'm *not* going to let you destroy that book. What will happen to Kolt and Robot Rabbit Boy? To humankind?"

Her brother's face flashed with savagery. "Who cares

about some dotty old Keeper and his tin-can animal freak. And human beings are like a disease that keeps spreading! Once the stupid Keepers can no longer return items to the world, the Losers will be in control of everything, even history itself, even the universe!"

"Those are Thrax's words, Gareth, not yours."

"So we're not following through with the plan?"

"You'd better get going before the villagers put you back in the snake pit."

Then Gertie had the most brilliant idea. "Join us! Come with us back to Skuldark."

Kolt looked concerned. "Um, what are you saying, Gertie? He's a Loser!"

"A dollop."

"But he can change!" Gertie insisted. "Like me. I was a Loser, and I changed."

"Seems like a very bad idea," Kolt said. "But then again, everyone deserves a second chance I suppose...."

"Please, Kolt!"

"Well..." he said, rubbing his chin in deep thought. "He *could* become Cave Sprite Manager, or a Fern Valley Ranger. I'm sure the B.D.B.U. would see the sense in it."

But Gertie's brother had backed away toward where his ship was hovering. "I can't," he said. "There's no way."

"Why not?" Gertie demanded, anger and hurt tearing through her. "Why?"

"Because Cava Calla Thrax saved us, and I can't betray him—even for you."

"Yes you can!" Gertie cried. "He was willing to let you get blown up with the B.D.B.U."

"But don't you see? If I double-cross him, we lose any chance to rescue our parents."

"Our parents?" Gertie said, flushing with panic and moving toward her brother and Doll Head. "You know where they are?"

"Thrax does! And if you destroy that book and come with me, we may be reunited with them! Will you come?"

Robot Rabbit Boy tried to run toward Gertie and pull her back, but Kolt stopped him. It had to be her choice.

No matter how much she wanted a family, she knew that her role as a Keeper of Lost Things was more important than the happiness of a few people, even if they were the people she loved. "Not like this . . ." she told herself. "We'll be together one day, Gareth. . . . But not like this."

When her brother saw that she had made up her mind, he was furious. "I'll *never* forgive you for betraying us! If Thrax lets our family die, it will be *your* fault!"

As though responding to his angry cry, Doll Head turned to face the three Keepers. At the sight of their hovering ship, and her brother's bitter face, Gertie felt one last burst of strength.

"There's no greater betrayal," she called out, "than when you betray yourself!"

Two neon light-nets dropped from Doll Head. One of them scooped up Gertie's brother, while the other just flapped about.

"Guess that was meant for me," she said to Kolt, who was now at her side with Robot Rabbit Boy.

Once Gareth Milk had been dragged up in the light beams and was onboard, Doll Head powered its engines, ready to depart, and the great flying head whizzed off into the sky.

"A dollop of eggcup!" snapped Robot Rabbit Boy, twitching his nose as though he were about to sneeze.

"No!" Gertie cried. "Let them go. He might be a Loser, but he's still my brother."

Kolt put his hand on her shoulder. "Well said, Gertie. Spoken like a true Keeper of Lost Things. Your parents would be proud of you."

With the disappearance of the flying head, the villagers began to cheer. Soon they would light fires and sing songs to celebrate their victory over fear and ignorance.

It would take time for Gertie to come to terms with everything she had found out.

"Why did you trust me, Kolt?" she asked, after they had eaten with the villagers, and were getting ready to go. "You must have suspected that Johnny the Guard Worm attacked me for a reason, and wondered why my name had been sewn onto the outside of my gown."

"It's true I had my fears."

"So then why were you so nice to me?"

"Because the only real weapon against a Loser, Gertie, or any person who lies and steals and hates and bullies, is genuine compassion. If I had treated you with suspicion and cruelty, it would only have made you worse. And besides, I thought you were excellent company. I just hoped I was wrong, and that you were a genuine Keeper who liked peach cake and moonberry juice—which it turns out you are, and do!"

"But why didn't you stand in my way before? I could have gone with him, back to Thrax to save our parents."

"You were chosen to be a Keeper for a reason. The B.D.B.U. does not make mistakes."

"You mean, it chooses very carefully whom to kidnap?"

Kolt chuckled, "I suppose that's true, but human civilization depends on it."

Before going home, Gertie and Kolt took the body of the brave Slug Lamp that Li Er had wrapped in silk. They would bury him under his favorite bush outside the cottage and place a giant golden moonberry to mark the spot. All the other Slug Lamps could look at it and remember him—that is, if Slug Lamps have memories.

"And after a cup of tea by the fire," Kolt said, "we should find a way to secure the door to the B.D.B.U. so this doesn't happen again. Thrax has become more powerful and more ruthless than I ever imagined."

Gertie agreed. "If he was willing to sacrifice my brother to destroy the B.D.B.U., then what else would he do?"

"We are entering dark times, I'm afraid, Gertie."

"Which is exactly why we're going to need help."

"Help? From whom?"

"All the Keepers we're going to rescue!"

"Keepers, rescue?"

"Lavender, eggcup?"

"Forget the Age of Disappearance, Kolt. This will be the Age of Gathering!"

"What do you mean?"

"A gathering of Keepers. I'll tell you more when we're back on Skuldark, but I already have a plan."

"Is it dangerous? Will I need my bowler hat?"

"I'm afraid it might be, and yes you will."

Kolt grinned. "Then count me in."

"Lavender!"

After saying goodbye to Er Dan, and his humble but brilliant son, the future Lao-tzu, they hugged Xiao Jian, and climbed onto the table with the B.D.B.U.

Just as they were linking up for the journey back to Skuldark, Gertie felt a sudden flash of hope and asked Kolt if they could go outside once more—in case her brother had changed his mind and was coming back.

But as the three friends huddled together in the darkness, all they could see was the brilliant light from stars, a glittering vastness where hope and fear would be forever bound.

Acknowledgments

The author would like to acknowledge the hard work, guidance, and friendship of Carrie Kania at Conville & Walsh Literary Agency; Katharine McAnarney and Lindsay Boggs, publicists at Penguin Young Readers; Kim Ryan, director, subsidiary rights at Penguin Young Readers; Alex Sanchez, editorial assistant at Razorbill; and Ben Schrank, president and publisher of Razorbill, and also my wonderful editor. The author would also like to recognize Tiffany Liao, who spent months camping on Skuldark, surviving on moonberries and peach cake, in order to make the story what it is today.